All Things New

Virtuous Heart Series

All Things New

BOOK ONE

Donna Fletcher Crow

Beacon Hill Press of Kansas City
Kansas City, Missouri

Copyright 1997
by Beacon Hill Press of Kansas City

ISBN 083-411-674X

Printed in the
United States of America

Cover design: Paul Franitza
Cover photo: Superstock

Library of Congress-in-Publication Data
Crow, Donna Fletcher.
    All things new / Donna Fletcher Crow.
      p.   cm. — (Virtuous heart series ; bk. 1)
    ISBN 0-8341-1674-X (pbk.)
    I. Title.   II. Series.
PS3553.R5872A79   1997
813'.54—dc21   97-13728
                                                   CIP

10 9 8 7 6 5 4 3 2 1

Therefore, if anyone is in Christ,
he is a new creation;
old things have passed away;
behold, all things have become new.
2 Cor. 5:17

Donna Fletcher Crow is a veteran author and speaker. She has written numerous works of fiction including *The Fields of Brannockburn*, *To Dust You Shall Return*, *A Gentle Calling*, *Treasures of the Heart*, and *The Castle of Dreams*. Awarded "First Place, Historical Fiction" in 1993 by the National Federation of Press Women for *Glastonbury*, Mrs. Crow is also the recipient of numerous other literary awards. She is the mother of four children and resides with her husband, Stanley, and daughter (still at home) in Boise, Idaho.

Chapter 1

The rolling waves of the Pacific Ocean washed the broad stretch of pale sand beyond the beach house. A thin line of gold and peach hung for a magic moment between sea and sky, then slipped into the water. Standing on the beach house deck, Debbie smiled. Why didn't the sea sizzle and boil when the sun sank into it?

Behind her the clink of ice in glasses and the bright, brittle laughter of her cousin's party called Debbie from her fantasy. She gripped the railing for just a moment. She had to go in. All those people having fun. She was supposed to be one of them. This was what life was supposed to be like. What hers would be like now. She lifted her chin and fixed a determined smile on her face. She could do it.

As she pushed her way through the waves of cacophony she thought of being 10 years old and going off the high diving board at swimming lessons. She had done it. She had survived. A stinging in her abdomen reminded her that she had belly flopped. But she had done it.

"And what do you want to be when you grow up, gorgeous?" The dark head of the man she had almost walked into loomed over Debbie. The pale contents of his glass sloshed dangerously as he spoke.

Debbie took a deep breath and selected an appetizer from the tray before her. This was the high diving board. A belly flop would be better than climbing down. "I'm going to be the first woman president. And don't you forget it." She flipped her dark hair and pushed her way further into the room, her long, floral skirt gently brushing her ankles. She found a relatively quiet corner by an open window and took a deep breath of the fresh salty air. But the shiver that followed wasn't entirely from the fact that even in mid-July the evenings were cool on the northern Oregon coast.

"There you are, darling! I might have known you'd be hiding yourself in the darkest corner available." Her cousin Byrl got a forceful grip on Debbie's arm and led her determinedly toward the milling guests. "I want you to meet this divine man—" Byrl interrupted herself with a giggle. "Oh, I guess that's sort of a pun—you see, he's a theologian. But never mind—he doesn't look the least bit dry and stuffy. You just never can tell about people, can you?"

Byrl interrupted her monologue to smile at a guest. The smile broke into splendor when she saw that the tall, red-headed woman was bearing a copy of Byrl's book. "Congratulations, Miss Coffman, your new book looks marvelous. Will you autograph it, please?"

While her cousin played gracious-guest-of-honor-and-noted-author, Debbie looked at the women around her. She had received introductions to most of the guests when they came in. She couldn't remember the names, but what each one did had been emphasized: photographer, interior decorator, lawyer, computer programmer . . . Well, they had made it in the "real world." So could she. Six years spent in a sheltered cocoon didn't have to determine her whole life.

"I just know you've got a best-seller here. The title is marvelous." Byrl's fan beamed at her freshly autographed book. *"If It Feels Good*—genius title. I love it!" She clutched the thick volume to her breast.

"Thank you. I do so hope that all my readers will find the book a liberating experience. As we go into a new millennium it's *terribly* important that we don't drag any *outmoded mores* with us. Each person finding her own values, listening to her own inner voice—" Byrl stopped and laughed at her own intensity. "Well, I won't climb up on my soapbox just now, but I *do* hope you enjoy the book." Byrl looked around blankly, as if trying to remember where she had mislaid something. "Oh, *Deborah.* Come along now, or we'll lose our quarry." They started to move, progressed at least three steps, and were interrupted again.

"Byrl, I want to take you to meet our new copy editor." Debbie recognized the lanky, silver-haired man in a black turtleneck as Hugh Parkinson, Byrl's publisher.

"Hugh, darling! What a *marvelous* party. And your new beach house is *fabulous*—what perfect timing to combine the launch of my book and your housewarming." Byrl kissed her publisher on the cheek.

"Yes, Judy in publicity was worried that people wouldn't be willing to drive out from Portland for the party. But I convinced her they'd drive from Portland, Maine, to meet Byrl Coffman."

Byrl laughed and kissed him again. "And to see Hugh Parkinson's new beach house." She linked her arm in his as they started to move away. "Debbie, *darling*, you'll forgive me for running off with Hugh. You'll be fine on your own. It's the Adonis by the bar—all golden and head-and-shoulders above everyone else." She pointed in a sweeping gesture to a man in a camel hair jacket. "Go introduce yourself."

The general movement of traffic was in the direction of the bar, and Debbie could hardly just stand there in the middle of the room, so she moved with the flow. What did Byrl expect her to do—go up and say, "Hello, Adonis. I'm Debbie. Byrl sent me"? Of course, that's exactly what Byrl would do.

"What can I get for you?"

Debbie started at the waiter's voice. She didn't realize she was already up to the bar. "Oh, do you have Mystic peach?"

The waiter turned to look over his collection of mineral waters. A hand gripped Debbie's left elbow. Even through her long-sleeved blouse it felt warm and slightly sticky. "We meet again, gorgeous. It must be karma." The man she had escaped earlier breathed on her neck. "Black hair, white skin, blue eyes . . . Mmmm, my favorite. What are you doing after the party?"

Debbie was rescued by the waiter asking, "Would you like anything in that?"

"May I suggest a sprig of mint?" The voice came from above Debbie's right shoulder. She looked up to see Byrl's Adonis-designate holding an icy drink with fresh green leaves floating in it.

"Why not?" She grinned. "Might as well splash out." That other man was still right behind her, so Debbie focused on the Adonis. "I think Byrl told me you publish with Parkinson too?"

"That's right; Parkinson House is broad-based if it's anything." His smile was ironic. "How about some fresh air?"

French doors led onto the side lawn where Japanese lanterns glowed red, gold, and green from the trees. Her companion was quiet, but Debbie didn't mind. It was a pleasant change not to be obligated to return bright chatter or to duck oily passes. They walked to the edge of the lawn and stood gazing out across the broad beach to where they could just see the rolling surf in the last of the silvery light. "You're a fan of Byrl Coffman, are you?" her companion asked.

"Oh, dear. Don't tell anyone, but I've never read any of her stuff. I'm her cousin. We're sharing a cottage just up the beach for the summer."

"Ah. And is that working out well?"

"It has to. I don't have anywhere else to go for the moment. I'm starting a new job in September, but until then . . ." She shrugged and walked slowly toward the beach. Her companion followed, several paces behind, apparently concentrating on his own thoughts. She appreciated the space he gave her as the panorama of rolling surf spreading before her drew her to reflect on the ebb and flow of life.

It was really incredible to contemplate that this was the first party she had attended in six years. When her mother first became ill she had given up all extracurriculars to help at home. Then her mother died, and she assumed the full brunt of raising Andy and Angie, her twin brother and sister, and keeping house for her father, who spent long hours working at the furniture store he owned in Boise. She had only taken time out to attend classes at the local university to earn her degree in fabric design. And somehow, six years had washed away in the channel of that sheltered flow.

But the ebb came suddenly, leaving no delightful tide pools of discovery, only barren beach. Angela married her high school sweetheart, Andy went off to college, and surprise of surprises—their father remarried. Debbie supposed most women of 24 would have been thrilled to be freed to a life of their own, but she was lost. She gave herself a little shake and took a sip of her drink.

"Welcome back," her contemplative companion greeted her.

"Oh, I guess I was rather far away. But I think you left first."

"Did I really? Sorry. I'm afraid that's an abominable habit of mine. I'll have to confess this isn't my kind of affair, but it's something of an occupational obligation. Let's start over." He held out his hand. "Hi. I'm Greg."

She hesitated. *It's only a handshake, for Pete's sake. What's the matter with you?* She got a firm grip on herself and offered her hand. "I'm Debbie Jensen. I—"

"Hello, *darlings!*" Byrl blew into their quiet circle. "I see you found each other." She eyed their fruit drinks. "I *knew* you'd suit. But I must warn you, Hugh is headed this way—I think he just unearthed a Buddhist or something for his resident theologian to cross swords with."

Greg groaned and turned to the call of duty.

"Well, now. Did I do you a favor or did I do you a favor?" Byrl gloated. "What did I tell you? Isn't he an Adonis?"

Debbie shrugged. "He's OK, I guess."

Byrl gave a gasp that was half astonishment, half contempt. "You're hopeless. I always *knew* too many years of homemaking would rot your mind."

Byrl turned from her impossible cousin to join a group whose minds worked more in harmony with her own. And this left Debbie free at last to escape back to the quiet cottage.

She had gone less than half a block along the Promenade, though, when she heard footsteps behind her. She slowed her pace, thinking that whoever it was would go on by. Then she gritted her teeth in frustration as her solitude was interrupted when the steps fell into pace with her own. She looked up at the tall dark man who had tried to pick her up earlier.

"Hello, Pretty Woman. How about letting Ryland Carlsburg escort you home?" Debbie turned to look at a dog scampering up the beach so she could pretend she didn't see the hand he extended. "You kept melting away at the party. I didn't want to miss a chance to get acquainted with the future first woman president."

Debbie groaned inwardly. Was she being punished for her flippancy? "Well, you'll have to arrange an interview with my campaign manager. I'm sure you'll understand. I found making my maiden speech exhausting."

Ryland smiled broadly and winked. "I'll follow up on that. I'm a firm believer in the policy of having friends in high places."

Bright chatter never came easily to Debbie, and this situation just didn't seem worth the effort. She walked on in silence toward the cottage.

Ryland became suddenly interested when he saw her accommodations. "Excellent location, isn't it? Pleasant walk to town. Are you enjoying the view?"

She shrugged. "It's fine. Byrl and I are just renting it for six weeks."

"And next year—how would you feel about staying in a luxury hotel on the same spot?"

"Luxury hotels aren't within my budget."

"Ah, but I can see that you get special rates. My company plans to build one right here. Seaside's been changing—slowly—the last 10 or 15 years. But now it's time for a whole new look—a whole new class of vacationer. And Ryburg Corp. will be at the head of it. Just as soon as we can get the medievalists on the city council to approve. You're not the only one with ambitions, Madam President."

She hurried up the front steps, but before she could reach the door Ryland Carlsburg picked up her hand and kissed it. He left her standing open-mouthed on the doorstep.

Debbie turned, trembling so hard she could hardly get her key out of her pocket. She fled to the bathroom and turned the taps on full blast. Making little choking noises in her throat, she scrubbed and scrubbed at her hand. She kept on until her skin was red and sore. There, that was enough. Now she could enjoy her bath—get rid of all the tensions the evening had created in her.

Turning from the sink, she filled the tub with steaming water and four capfuls of Byrl's aromatherapy herbal wash. She yanked her clothes off, so anxious to get in the water she hardly noticed that she pulled the top button off her blouse in the process. Ahhh. She lay back in the water, soaking her hair as well.

Gradually she began to relax. And the dark cloud of depression that she had hoped the party would chase away rolled over her. How could she have failed so badly? She had been so determined. She was intelligent, healthy, well-educated, reasonably attractive, only 24 years old. There was no reason she couldn't make a new life—be a new her. She had lived like a nun in a convent for 6 years. But there was no reason she couldn't put that behind her. Achieve her own identity. All those bright, successful women at the party had done it.

And after all, she had already landed a dream of a job.

She was incredibly lucky to be promised the position of fabric designer and teacher at Rainbow Land when the woman now in that position left. What else could possibly fit her education and all those years of experience sewing at home so well? But had she left home too precipitously?

Byrl's invitation to share a beach cottage had seemed like a godsend. Her nomadic cousin needed a quiet place to turn out the series of columns on two centuries of women in America, which she had sold to *Working Woman* magazine. And Debbie needed a transition home before she moved to her own apartment and started work. She would have felt like a chaperone on a honeymoon staying with her father and his new bride—even though they had assured her she would be welcome.

As she looked back over the evening, though, Debbie couldn't help but wonder if the whole idea had been a terrible mistake. What was wrong with her? Why couldn't she go to a party and have a good time like any other woman? If she couldn't even go to a book launching party, could she hold down a responsible, creative job? Would she be able to break out of the cocoon she had sheltered in for so long?

She was still asking herself those same questions when she slipped into her flannel granny gown and pulled her quilt up to her chin. She had been asleep only a short time when the dream came again. *Dolls. Beautiful, golden-curled baby dolls with blue eyes. Soft, delicate peachy skin. But then they started to cry. Cry and twist. And break. Broken dolls. Pieces floating and writhing. The cries increased to screams.*

She sat up, her face wet. The screams were her own.

But even awake, the cries didn't stop. And the broken dolls continued to contort in her mind. What was wrong with her? She must be losing her mind.

She reached for one of the little white tablets her doctor had given her when she told him about her sleeping problems. *Make them work. Please. Just for tonight.*

Chapter 2

Debbie drew back the seafoam green drapes covering the picture window that looked out over the wide expanse of the Pacific Ocean. Dr. Hilde's pill had done its work, and Debbie had finally slept so soundly she hadn't even heard Byrl come in from the party. Byrl would sleep for hours yet. But Debbie loved the misty early mornings. She felt cozy, protected. Back in her cocoon.

She nestled in her quilted bathrobe in a corner of the sofa, sipping coffee from a mug, the fat *Sunday Oregonian* unopened on the coffee table. Before her the white-edged, silvery waves washed the pale sand with their eternal rhythm beneath a blue-gray sky. The whole scene was scrimmed with a light haze like a soft-focus photograph. Near the water's edge two early strollers followed at a leisurely pace behind a large, bounding dog, while an occasional seagull swooped down to settle on the concrete balustrade of the beachfront Promenade.

Relishing the scene before her, Debbie was glad Ryland Carlsburg hadn't constructed his luxury hotel on the spot yet. She hoped he never would. But then she shouldn't be so selfish. Just think how many more people could be enjoying this scene in a hotel offering the same vista that the five cottages on this lot enjoyed. But still—it wouldn't be the same . . .

The clock on the mantel whirred and clunked—any ability it once possessed to chime had long since departed. But the oddly endearing sounds left a crack in Debbie's refuge. It was time to get ready for church. Time to face a new situation. Time to meet a roomful of new people. Well, she had survived last night's party—barely. Church couldn't be half that bad.

A short time later Debbie drove the 11 miles through beautiful green woodland to Cannon Beach, still arguing with herself. It was ridiculous to feel threatened by the thought of going to church. What place could be safer? And why was she worrying about safety anyway? She should be excited about this new experience. She was going to attend morning worship at a world-famous Bible study center. She had heard of the Cannon Beach Conference all her life. Besides, she never missed church. It was odd, really. But it seemed that the more cut off from God she felt, the more necessary church attendance seemed to be.

She turned in at the conference grounds between two tall brick columns and surveyed the layout of the freshly painted, brick-red buildings with crisp, white trim. Which one was the chapel? Debbie glanced nervously at her watch. Going into a roomful of strangers was bad enough. Going in late was unthinkable.

Several people were entering a long, low building across the grounds. That must be it. As Debbie hurried forward, banks of colorful flowers flourishing around the green plush carpet of grass cheered her on. Masses of yellow marigolds, red salvia, white alyssum, and intensely purple velvet petunias made a joyfully welcoming kaleidoscope. And offered the comfort of home. Debbie's flower garden had always been her greatest joy. She loved growing things, nurturing tiny green shoots and seeing them flower into mature beauty. And she would never give up on the weakest, most forlorn seedling. I'll just give it a chance, she would think. And she was often rewarded for her care.

Debbie slipped into a back seat of the chapel just as they were finishing the first hymn. The next hymn was followed by announcements of the week's activities: seminars on music and theology, family camp, women's Bible study, teen beach service this afternoon, this evening a special reception in honor of Mrs. Adelaide Masefield, who would be their guest for the last night of the conference . . . As the list continued, Debbie looked around her. She liked the cozy feeling of the natural woods and red carpet. And at the front, two tall, narrow stained-glass windows reflected the work of the Creator with a design of flowers, trees, and sky.

Her attention returned to the speaker as he introduced their special guest for the morning, head of the theology department of Pacific Evangelical Seminary in Portland. "His credits are many, including the fact that he received his Ph.D. from Harvard Divinity School and is still an Evangelical— which has to be proof of a firm foundation . . ."

The audience laughed. Debbie shifted in her seat and crossed her legs. Why did announcements and introductions have to take up so much time? Who cared about the biography of some ancient academician? "He is the author of *Joy in the Mourning, Dealing with Guilt and Grief,* and *A Little Lower than the Angels* . . ." The list went on. Debbie crossed her legs the other way. ". . . and on top of all his other activities, he is a well-known television guest personality. So we are delighted to present to you this morning, Dr. Gregory Masefield."

Debbie's purse slid to the floor, where it lay unretrieved. Her head came up, her lips parted, and she blinked rapidly several times to be sure that the tall blond man standing in the pulpit was really the same man she had met at a cocktail party the night before. No wonder he had been as uncomfortable in those circumstances as she had. She kept wanting to blink her ears to be sure it was the same voice. He had seemed so quiet and soft-spoken last night. The man in the pulpit spoke with such authority. He was dynamic without ever raising his voice. His text was "Created in the image of God," and he laid out clearly what it meant to be created in the image of the Creator and how this should carry over into one's respect for human life and one's love for all people as God's children. His knowledge of the Scriptures amazed her, as he quoted extensive passages without using notes or looking anything up. He ended with Deuteronomy 30:19, "I have set before you life and death . . . therefore choose life."

The congregation stood for a closing hymn and prayer. Debbie looked down at her hands and realized she had shredded the bulletin she had been holding. It was incredibly cold in the room. And yet her forehead was beaded with perspiration. Why did she keep going to church when the experience always made her feel so guilty? Besides, what did she have to feel guilty about? She believed in God. She believed she was going to heaven. It was just getting through this life that was the problem.

She ducked quickly out the side door. She had no desire to offer a smiling handshake and bright compliments to the speaker. She wanted to get in her car and lock the doors. And drive back to Seaside very, very slowly. Maybe Byrl would be gone and she could be alone.

One tug on the locked car door reminded her. Her purse still lay where it had fallen on the floor of the chapel. By the time she walked back across the grounds, the sanctuary was almost empty. Only a cluster of people remained, gathered around the morning's speaker. She slipped in quietly, found her purse quickly, and was almost to the exit when a familiar voice stopped her. "Deborah Jensen. I thought that was you in the congregation. Wish I'd known you were a believer last night, I'd have taken you along to help me out with Hugh's Buddhist."

"I wouldn't have been much help—and I can't imagine you needing any." It seemed as though she should say something more. They stood by the open door where a blindingly bright bed of red and yellow flowers caught her eye. "The conference center is beautiful—especially the gardening."

"Have you seen the beach here—Haystack Rock? Now *that's* impressive."

She shook her head. "No. This is my first visit to the Oregon coast."

He looked at his watch. "It's an hour yet until dinner is

served . . . there's time to take a quick look. You haven't been to the Oregon coast if you haven't seen Haystack Rock."

Debbie considered. Her first impulse was to mumble an excuse and run to her car. But no. She took a firm grip on herself. She had come here determined to break old habits, to build a new life. She was silly even to consider declining.

"Sure. I'd love to. Want to take my car? It's just over there in the lot."

"Great. I have to pick up my daughter first. She's in the children's program across the way." He gestured to another big red building on the far side of the grounds.

But Debbie's eyes didn't follow the pointing right hand, they flew instead to his left where, indeed, a plain gold band encircled the third finger. Did the fact he was married make him safer or more dangerous? Silly. Why should such questions come into the situation at all? They were only going to look at the beach, for goodness' sake. Still, it took her a moment to adjust her thinking. So why had Byrl pushed her at him if he were married? Probably because Byrl considered any man fair game. Byrl didn't know anything about him anyway, except that Parkinson House published his books, which were highly respected.

Debbie suddenly realized he was waiting for her reply. "Oh, sure. Fine. What's your daughter's name?"

"Melissa. She's six. They have an excellent children's program here. She's had a great week."

"How nice."

And Debbie kept repeating that over and over to herself as they entered the colorfully decorated children's building. Nice. It was nice that Gregory Masefield had a daughter. It was nice that Melissa could go to the beach with them. Melissa was a nice little girl. So why did it require such effort to keep from backing away from the child? Why was it such an effort to smile at her?

Melissa was as blond as her daddy, but no one could accuse her of having his inclination toward being quiet. She flew into his arms from across the room and giggled as he swung her to the dizzying heights above his head. Back on the ground, she tied the bows on the lace-edged white sunbonnet that matched her organdy pinafore dress and squealed with delight when her daddy informed her of the plan to go to the beach.

At the car, Debbie handed her keys to Greg. "You drive. You know where we're going." She was no more than settled in the passenger seat, however, than Melissa started to climb onto her lap. Debbie let out a little gasp and scooted as far to the side as her seat belt would allow. Apparently the child was accustomed to sitting in her mother's lap. So where was she, anyway?

"Not today, Punkin." Greg pulled his daughter back. "I want you in your own seat with your own seat belt." He deposited Melissa on the backseat and buckled her belt. Debbie relaxed.

Greg followed a narrow, winding road that led away from town and up a steep hill. Near the top of the hill he parked. They walked the short distance to the crest of the hill, serenaded by the faint tinkle of wind chimes from the deck of a beach house and Melissa's light, little-girl voice as she danced between them.

"Oh!" At the top of the hill Debbie stood transfixed. Even though she was wearing sunglasses, she put her hands up to shade her eyes. The brilliant light shot through the clear sea air and flung handfuls of gleaming diamonds across the blue-white waters and the silvery sands.

"Magnificent, isn't it?" Beside her, Greg surveyed the scene. "It takes everyone like that. When Merriweather Clark saw it, he recorded in his journal that he had beheld the grandest and most pleasing prospect that his eyes ever surveyed."

"Clark? As in Lewis and Clark?" Debbie struggled to recall her Northwest history lessons. "I didn't know they were here."

"This whole coast is Lewis and Clark country. They call it the edge of history. Did you notice the sculpture back there?"

Debbie tore her gaze from the panorama before her to look where Greg indicated. A wire sculpture of the buckskin-clad explorers, led by Sacajawea, their Indian guide, stood surveying the view that Captain Clark had so much admired almost 200 years before. "It's perfect, isn't it?"

"As if they were still standing there," Greg agreed.

Then Debbie turned again to look at the view the statue was enjoying. Landmark Haystack Rock stood sentinel in the waves with a mist at its feet. To the left, layer after layer of rugged coastal mountains, ethereal with banks of mist hanging between them, stood stacked one behind the other like cardboard cutouts for an elaborate stage setting.

Greg took a step forward. His arm brushed hers. She moved away. "Haystack is one of the world's largest freestanding monoliths and a protected wildlife sanctuary. Seagulls, puffins—all kinds of birds nest on it, and the base is covered with sea creatures. You can walk out to it when the tide's—"

"Daddy, Daddy!" Melissa's voice floated to them from the beach below. "Listen. I can make the sand squeak!" She began moving in a wide circle, dragging her feet.

"We're coming." Greg led the way down the steep, wooden steps to the beach. Debbie pulled off her shoes and tossed them beside Melissa's abandoned white patent Mary Janes. Laughing, she followed Melissa around her circle, pushing her feet down hard with each step for maximum effect. Greg stepped out of his shoes and joined them. His larger feet produced an even louder sound. "They call it 'singing sands.'"

"They might call it that, but it sounds like squeaking to me." Debbie abandoned the circle to squeak her way toward the water. "Since you're so well informed, why do they call it Cannon Beach? Is one of the rocks shaped like a cannon?"

"Good guess, but actually it's named for a cannon that washed ashore here. A schooner shipwrecked on Tillamook Head before the lighthouse was built."

Bored with making the sands sing, Melissa danced on toward the ocean. Debbie watched as the child began playing tag with the waves, keeping just a jump ahead of them as they rolled up on the sand, then chasing them back out to sea where they belonged. Debbie stood frozen. The pain around her heart was so sharp she couldn't move. The little sprite, dressed in white organdy, danced with freedom and delight like a bit of seafoam herself. Debbie couldn't stand to watch. But she couldn't pull her eyes away. And she couldn't understand the ache inside her.

Did the scene recall some forgotten memory? Had she once danced like this on a beach while her mother watched? Was she now, six years later, feeling grief for her mother's early death? Or was she losing her mind? The painful void she felt inside was the same she experienced when she woke from her anguished nightmares. She had told her doctor about them, and all he had been able to suggest was the Trezadone. But she had no pills now. She had never before needed one in the middle of the day.

At last a hubbub of noise and motion down the beach moved her attention from the oddly distressing scene. A cluster of horseback riders approached, laughing and chattering, the metal on their harnesses ringing above the noise of the surf. They were riding in the wettest part of the sand where the horses could have the firmest footing, so Greg and Debbie moved back to the dry, warm, squeaky sand to let them pass. For perhaps two or three minutes their view of the sprite-child dancing in the waves was blocked by the broadside of horseflesh.

When the view cleared, Melissa was not in sight.

"Melissa!" Greg shouted and darted forward.

He was answered by a wailing shriek from what appeared to be a clump of sandy seaweed left by the retreating wave. Forgetful of his crisp white shirt and suit pants, he scooped the sodden bundle into his arms and cradled her securely.

"The horses were in the way. The wave got me." Melissa's words came out in frightened sobs.

"Don't worry, Punkin. You're safe now." Her daddy smoothed the tangled hair back from the child's brow and carefully wiped the sand off her face. Then he bent and kissed a smooth round cheek before turning toward the car.

Debbie turned to follow, but her knees buckled under her. She was sitting on the warm sand of a sunny beach, but she saw only blackness. Blackness with red streaks. And the floating, twisted pieces of dismembered dolls. She was awake, but the nightmare held her. The cries of the broken dolls mingled with Melissa's sobs and Greg's shouting "Melissa!" And then Debbie realized the shout had been her own.

"Debbie. What is it? Melissa's OK." Greg knelt beside her, one arm holding his daughter, the other around Debbie's shoulder. "You sounded terrified. Don't worry. Melissa had a bad fright, but she's fine. Aren't you, Punkin?"

Debbie shook her head. What had happened? What must he think of her? She scrambled unsteadily to her feet. "No, I— That is, I don't know what happened. I have this sort of nightmare . . ."

Greg held her arm to steady her. "What is it? Were you frightened by horses or water or something as a kid?"

"I—I don't remember. But that sounds logical." *Oh please, let it be something logical.*

Greg led the way back up the beach. "That makes sense. If you were frightened as badly as you sounded, you likely wouldn't remember it."

"Really? Is that true?" *Was there hope? A rational explanation?* They started right after her mother's death. Dr. Hilde thought that was what caused them. But Debbie feared it was something worse. "Certainly. It's quite normal for the subconscious to suppress something that's too painful for the conscious mind to deal with. The trouble is, it can't stay suppressed forever. Someday the pain or fear will have to come out and be dealt with. Do you think you might have almost drowned as a child?"

"I don't know. No one ever mentioned it. How can I deal with something I don't even know happened?"

"You can't. You need to ask your parents."

Debbie shook her head. "Not easy. My mother died six years ago. My dad's on his honeymoon."

"Brothers? Sisters?"

"One of each. Twins. They're four years younger, though. They might not know. I'll ask Dad when he gets home." Just the thought that there could be help, that her reactions could be "normal" was the most freeing thing Debbie had ever felt. She could have flung out her arms and raced up the beach. *Yes, yes, yes! Let it be true. Please.*

Chapter 3

"Mmmm, there's something to be said for having Miss American Homemaker for a roommate—I never lived around a kitchen that *smelled so good* before. It's a *great* way to beat the Monday evening blahs. What *is* it?"

Debbie smiled. Even a day spent at the computer didn't dampen Byrl's habit of speaking in italics. "Salmon soufflé with cucumber sauce."

"Sounds *divine*. Where'd you learn how to do all this?"

Debbie shrugged and began arranging clusters of green grapes and slices of pale orange cantaloupe on a plate. "Practice. I once cooked my way through the entire Time-Life *Foods of the World* series, until Angela discovered she'd gained four pounds and threw a fit. Then she went on some ridiculously restricted diet, so I had to try to concoct tasty dishes from a list of about seven allowable foods. I got pretty good at it."

When the buzzer sounded, she carefully opened the oven door and gently nudged the soufflé pan with a mitted hand. "Too much shimmy. Another seven minutes. You can wash the salad greens."

"Who, me?" Byrl made a face. "You forget I'm liberated from all that."

"Yeah, you'll be liberated to McDonald's. Wash."

Byrl good-naturedly picked up a bunch of leaf lettuce and turned to the sink. "I just can't get over it. You really *like* the homemaking bit, don't you?"

"I loved the feeling of running a tight ship. I filled the house with beautiful music, delicious food, and happy people. What could possibly be more fulfilling?"

Byrl shook her head as she flipped the green leaves under running water. "I thought that kind of thinking went out in the '60s—the 1860s."

"Well, if it did, it's time for a resurgence. I hope I can accomplish something of the sort with the classes I'll be teaching."

"Making curtains—*fulfilling!*"

"So I'm a dinosaur. I warned you. Call the museum."

"The asylum is more likely."

Debbie started at her cousin's jibe, then realized it was only banter. She had been so happy all day. And she wasn't going to let anything spoil it. She had slept perfectly last night without—

"Yeech!" Byrl's shriek interrupted her reverie. "There's sand coming *up* the drain!" Byrl dropped the lettuce and jumped back in disgust.

"Oh, no." Debbie set her fruit plate on the table. "I thought I had that fixed. Get the plunger from the bathroom closet, will you? And hurry. The soufflé falls in four minutes."

Byrl was quick with the plunger, but despite Debbie's best efforts, the suction action of the plunger served only to bring up more sand and sludge—and a foul smell with it. "Any ideas?" Debbie's voice held a note of desperation. "Where do you call a plumber after six o'clock?" The black slime was now creeping over the edge of the sink.

"When I rented this place the agent said there would be a resident landlord in the cottage next door. I haven't seen anyone around, but I suppose it's worth a try." Byrl started for the door.

"Right." Debbie stepped around the puddle forming on the floor and made another assault with the plunger. "See if you can rouse somebody. I'll keep at this and pray for the soufflé."

Her heart sank, however, when the buzzer sounded a minute later. The soufflé tested a perfect doneness. But the kitchen smelled like tar and leaf mold. And the ooze was still rising. They couldn't possibly eat her delicate dish in the midst of this mess. She turned the oven off, left the door open a crack, and hoped for the best. Behind her the sink began making gurgling sounds.

Feeling like a coward deserting under fire she turned and fled—right into the arms of Gregory Masefield.

"Whoa." He grinned at her gasp and put his hands on her shoulders to steady her. "I do keep turning up like a bad penny, don't I?"

Debbie was too amazed to say anything. She backed away from his touch, wondering where on earth Byrl had found him. She was certain someone had said that conference ended yesterday.

Greg took one look at the stinking muck. "Well, it's a wise man who knows when he's outclassed. That sink wins hands down. Courtenay left me a list of emergency phone numbers. I'll be right back." And he was gone.

Debbie stood blinking at the door. "Did I really see who I think I saw?"

"Isn't it just *too marvelous!*" Byrl flung out her arms. "That, my dear, is our landlord. Or, at least, he answered the door at the landlord's cottage, and Courtenay Wallace was the agent's name—so he must be on the level."

"But he's some great Ph.D. brain, not a handyman."

"Of course. That's why he's calling for help instead of standing knee deep in that yuck brandishing a monkey wrench. Don't tell *me* he didn't learn anything at school."

In a few minutes Greg returned with a plumber in tow. He pointed the man in the direction of the kitchen and turned to Byrl and Debbie. "Well, the least your landlord can do is take you out for a bowl of clam chowder while Charlie puts everything to rights." Sloshing noises from the kitchen told them that the competent Charlie was already hard at work. "Judging from the clean dishes on the table, it looks like your dinner died an untimely death."

Debbie gasped. "My soufflé!" then she shrugged. "Might as well go out. I'll give it a decent burial when we get home." She covered the fruit platter and salad greens and stepped across Charlie's tools to put them in the refrigerator.

A few minutes later they were headed down the boardwalk along the beach to town with Melissa in a pink jogging suit dancing ahead of them. Debbie turned to Greg. "Now, tell us how this came about. How you came about—being here."

"My sister's real estate agency in Portland manages these beach houses. Courtenay and her husband usually live here themselves in the summer; it makes a nice break for them. But this year Fred's engineering firm had some big project going he couldn't get away from, and Court is in the middle of expanding her agency, so they needed a substitute here. I was doing the stint at Cannon Beach last week anyway and don't have to be back on campus until after Labor Day. Sooo . . . I thought it sounded easy. She didn't tell me the part about the plumbing. I have a feeling Charlie and I are going to become very good friends this summer."

It was a pleasant walk to town, beachfront hotels lining the way on their left and the wide, smooth Seaside beach to their right, with the impressive cloud-topped Tillamook Head jutting out into the ocean in front of them. Byrl and Greg chatted about their current writing projects. Debbie tried to concentrate on the scenery. But her attention kept straying to the little girl bouncing in front of them, her soft blond hair tossing in the breeze and her sneakers flashing red and gold lights with every step—a delightful sight. So why did it make her want to burst into tears?

She was relieved when they reached the Turnaround where Seaside's main street met the Promenade. The historical marker offered a safe focus. "End of the Lewis and Clark Trail, January 2, 1806," she read aloud.

"Are you including Sacajawea in your sketches of American women?" Greg asked Byrl.

"Oh! What a *super* idea!" She hugged him impulsively.

"Thank you, Darling! How *could* I have missed her?" Byrl pulled out the notebook she always carried in her pocket and jotted a note.

They turned down Broadway, walking past the Sand Dollar Square shops, and turned up Columbia to a gray-blue building with a lighthouse-shaped cupola. "This must be good." Debbie surveyed the long row of patrons standing in line along the covered walkway.

"Only problem is, once you've eaten Norma's clam chowder you're spoiled for life." Greg took a place at the end of the line.

"Daddy, can we ride the bumper cars after dinner? Please?" Melissa tugged at her daddy's hand.

He grinned. "Sounds like a good idea. We'll see."

The line moved steadily forward, but for every advance another group joined the line behind them, so the queue was never shorter than the building itself. Melissa tugged at the edge of Debbie's white nylon jacket. "Do you like to ride bumper cars?"

"Well, I don't know. I've never done it."

The round blue eyes grew wide in astonishment. "Oh, it's the funnest thing in the world." And she proceeded, with uninhibited gestures, to demonstrate a bumper car ride. Debbie made herself listen. And smile. In spite of the burning sensation in her throat.

By the time Melissa's narrative was exhausted, they were almost to the door of the restaurant. Debbie turned to find her gregarious cousin making friends with the group behind them.

"Deb, this is George and Sylvia from Eugene *and* their friend Alex. Sylvia recognized me from the cover of my book. Isn't that *exciting!*"

Everyone beamed agreement that it was, indeed, exciting—especially the tall, dark Alex, whose crisp mustache accented his deep tan. Before Debbie could reply, Byrl and Alex were again deep in conversation. As they moved to the front of the line, Byrl said, "You dears go ahead and get a table for three. Alex has invited me to join them." She leaned close to Debbie and spoke in an exaggerated whisper. "He has some politically incorrect ideas you wouldn't *believe*. I simply must set him straight." Byrl's eyes flashed a crusading gleam. But Debbie wasn't so certain that the gleam in Alex's eyes had anything to do with political opinion.

"Chowder all around?" Greg inquired when they were seated. Debbie nodded and Melissa clapped her hands. The salad came first, crisp greens topped with tiny, plump, pink shrimp and a tasty dressing; then steaming bowls of creamy clam chowder, each with its own sun pool of melted butter.

Debbie savored her first mouthful. "Ooh, what I'd give for this recipe. I have Abigail Adam's secret for clam chowder—she cooked soda crackers in it for thickening."

Greg's brow wrinkled in surprise. "I didn't realize a woman of your ambitions would be interested in cooking."

"What do you know about my ambitions? I—" but before she could finish, Melissa tugged at her daddy's sleeve and whispered in his ear. Greg nodded and started to rise. "I'll take her," Debbie offered.

Greg sat back, looking eminently relieved. "Thanks. Public rest rooms are a major disadvantage of being a daddy." Debbie glanced at the gold band on his finger and wanted to ask, "So where's the mommy?" Debbie knew something about mommies that abandoned their families. She felt a wave of anger on behalf of all little girls left without anyone to see to their needs.

But no, there had been some reference to a Mrs. Masefield at the conference. She was probably still there. She was sure to show up in a day or two since they were neighbors. Debbie hurried across the room after Melissa.

Debbie was staring at the seashell wallpaper when Melissa came out to wash her hands. She stood in front of the sink. "I need a boost."

Debbie jumped. "Oh, of course." But instead of picking

up the child she simply turned on the taps so Melissa could stick her hands under the running water.

"Do you have any little girls?" Melissa asked as she took the paper towel Debbie held out to her.

"No."

"Why not?"

"Well, I have a sister."

"Don't you want a little girl?"

"Come on. Our chowder will be cold."

When they all finished licking their bowls clean, Greg suggested Norma's homemade apple cobbler, but Debbie really was too full, so she just drank coffee while Greg enjoyed his dessert. "You must be proud of your cousin," Greg observed after Debbie caught Byrl's eye at a nearby table and smiled at her. "She's a very accomplished woman."

"Oh, yes. She has done well, hasn't she?" She could think of nothing else to say on the subject, so she asked, "And your sister has her own business?"

"Yes, Courtenay's agency is small, but they're very successful. She built it all by herself in less than five years." His voice reflected unmistakable pride in his sister. "Real estate was a natural for her because she always loved houses. She specializes in older homes and makes a great many of her sales because she has such a good eye for how they can be fixed up. She draws these exciting verbal pictures and gets her clients just itching to make the dream a reality—and of course, they have to buy the house as a first step."

"That's great. It's too bad she's not closer to Boise. She'd be a good person to speak to my classes on using fabrics in interior design."

"Oh, is that what you do? I thought you were serious about the political thing."

Debbie set her coffee cup down. "Oh, dear. Is that bit of flippancy going to haunt me forever?"

Greg shook his head. "It's forgotten already. Tell me about the real you."

She shrugged. "Not much to tell—six years keeping house for Dad and the twins."

"And you were so successful that you worked yourself out of a job."

"What a great way to put it!"

"And now you're out to conquer new horizons."

"Absolutely." And she lifted her chin and shook her dark hair to assure herself that she meant it. It sounded so easy when you said it like that. And apparently it was. For other women. What was the matter with her?

"Now can we ride the bumper cars, Daddy?" Melissa had waited with surprising patience until the last bite of apple cobbler disappeared into her daddy's mouth, then, like a kitten waiting to pounce, she didn't hesitate long enough for him to swallow.

He smiled, nodded, and swallowed all at once. "Sure, Punkin. If our friend here thinks her digestion can take such rough treatment."

"I'm game." Debbie jumped to her feet.

Greg, who had vacationed at Seaside since childhood, explained that the Scooters were one of the landmarks of the resort. "Down at that end where the silver foil paper is, there used to be cartoon characters of Maggie and Jiggs—from the '50s at least—Maggie towered over her poor, henpecked husband declaring, 'Jiggs, I want to ride too.' I thought it was a shame they ever covered them up. But then, I'm a sucker for nostalgia."

"So you're not necessarily in favor of all the uptown expansion being proposed around here?"

"Not much chance they'll get too carried away. Oregon has some of the toughest land-use planning legislation in the nation." Greg turned to fold his long legs into the little red car Melissa had chosen and buckled his daughter in beside him.

Debbie chose a yellow one. All the scooters soon filled, the bell rang, and Debbie pushed her accelerator to the floor. With shrieks of laughter from the drivers, the colorful little beetles took off after each other around and around the big silver room: bumping, bouncing, careening into traffic jams that would make a Los Angeles freeway look like a back-country road. The only rule was no head-on collisions, and even then a few occurred to cars spun around in the melee.

Debbie's attack instincts were not as highly developed as many of the others. She preferred to drive a wide swath around the pack and challenge herself to see if she could complete a circle without getting bumped. She was almost around her second circuit when a thumping push from the rear accompanied with delighted little-girl laughter told her a battle was on.

She purposely slowed down, forcing them to pass her. Then she accelerated on the corner and accomplished a beautiful broadside shove. Greg shook his fist for revenge. Debbie shrieked in mock terror.

All too soon the bell rang. The cars drifted to a stand-still, the shaft each one sported like a pointer hound's tail, no longer receiving power from the electrified metal ceiling. "Let's go again, Daddy! Please, can we?" Greg grinned and handed the attendant the money. Melissa wriggled out of her seat belt and darted across the floor. "I'll ride with you this time." She climbed into Debbie's car.

Debbie instinctively edged closer to her own side. But she had no choice. She reached over and snapped Melissa's seat belt.

The bell rang and they were off. Fluorescent lights around the walls and glimmering headlights from the little cars reflected off the metal floor and ceiling and silver wall-paper. The room was vibrant with shine and motion. Debbie's laughter matched Melissa's, and they waved wildly to their reflections in the mirror that covered the back wall.

"Get Daddy!" Melissa shouted. Debbie took off, driving her craziest and shrieking with Melissa when their goal was accomplished with a bump that sent him spinning. Then he returned the compliment.

Still laughing, and with her knees weak from the wild ride, Debbie was glad for Greg's arm to help her from the car when the bell sounded again. But she was surprised that he didn't immediately let go when she was once again on firm ground. She pulled away.

As they walked back up Broadway to the beach, the sun slipped beneath the horizon, leaving behind it a gentle peach, apricot, and lavender tinted sky. People walking along the water's edge made sharp silhouettes against the pale background. Down the beach a few fires winked into life as groups gathered around the big logs washed ashore by the winter sou'westers. Melissa ran down the wide stairs from the Turnaround to the sand and made a beeline for the swings. "Give me a start," she requested of Debbie. "I can pump, but it's hard to get started."

Debbie gave her three good pushes. When she saw the little legs firmly catch the rhythm, she took the empty swing seat next to Melissa and matched her motion to the child's.

"'How do you like to go up in a swing?'" Debbie's voice rose with their bodies on the word *up*. "'Up in the air so blue—Oh, I do think it the pleasantest thing ever a child can do. Up in the air and over the wall—'" She stopped. "No, that won't do. 'Up in the air and over the *beach*—till I can see so wide, ocean and mountains and sand and all over the countryside. Till I look down on the *beach so white*, down on the *pale blue sea*. Up in the air I go flying again, up in the air, and down."

"Oh, I liked it!" Melissa cried. "Did you make it up?"

"Goodness no." Debbie laughed. "A man named Robert Louis Stevenson wrote it in Scotland over a hundred years ago. I just adapted it a bit. My mother always said it to me when I was little. And I always thought someday . . ." Her voice strangled in her throat. Her legs quit pumping and her hands dug into the heavy chains of the swing.

How many years had it been since she had thought of that experience? There had been a giant old cottonwood tree in their backyard with a rope swing in it. She had loved that swing. She would sit in it by the hour, telling herself stories. And she would twist the ropes round and round, then lift her feet and let the world spin around and around. And she could remember laying her head back until she was level with the swing seat and holding on for dear life. Around and around. She must have been about Melissa's age.

And then her mother would come out from the kitchen and push her. High. So high she could almost touch the leaves with her toes. And her mother would recite Robert Louis Stevenson. How could she have forgotten that? The memory brought a tumult of emotions with it. Undefined, puzzling emotions.

"Do you know any more?" Melissa's voice was breathless, her legs kicking higher and higher.

Debbie pushed herself forward. After three or four sweeps of the lulling motion, the agitation inside her calmed. The breeze blew against her face, pushing her back. The waves rose and fell beyond the stretch of sand. Her own rhythmic breathing steadied her.

"More? Well, I should. Let me think." Yes, there had been dozens of rhymes. Sitting on her mother's lap, going places together in the car, walking along sidewalks covered with crunchy leaves. The flood of memories almost choked her.

Debbie took a deep breath. Could she do this without her voice breaking? "To market, to market, to buy a fat pig, / home again, home again, jiggety-jig. / To market, to market . . ." She completed three verses without a hesitation. ". . . home again, home again, market is done."

Melissa giggled with delight and kicked her feet. Then she leaned back until her body was level, her hands gripping the chain high above—just as Debbie had remembered doing herself so many years ago.

The peach and apricot slid from the sky, leaving an ever-darkening gray overhead. More and more fires twinkled up and down the length of the sand. "Time to go, Punkin." Melissa obeyed her father without demur. Rather than going back up to the Prom, they walked to the water and strolled along the edge of the damp sand where the footing was firmer, with Melissa, as usual, dancing circles around the adults. Then she dashed off to join a group gathered to watch a man and boy flying a radio-controlled model plane.

"Does she ever run down?" Debbie asked above the sound of the surf and the buzzing of the plane.

"I can hope. I always think something like a romp in the fresh air will make her easier to get to bed, but I'm afraid I tire out first."

Again, Debbie wondered about the wife and mother that would leave such responsibilities. Daughters needed their mothers. What if something happened? Something the daughter couldn't cope with?

Debbie must have still been thinking about such questions when she went to bed that night because she dreamed about her own mother. Herself and her mother, in the car, and her mother was laughing and quoting a nursery rhyme to her.

But then it wasn't her mother. It was herself. And she was saying poems to Melissa. Shouting them, shrieking them, over and over between bouts of shrill laughter as the bumper car spun round and round. And then there were streaks of red paint slashed across the foil paper. And cartoon characters cavorting across the ceiling. And then the scooters piled up, and all the dolls and cartoons ripped and broke.

And Melissa was in there somewhere. Somewhere under the pile of scooters and shattered dolls. Debbie dug and dug through the wreckage, crying and shouting her name, and the name of all the Mother Goose characters—Jack and Jill, and little Boy Blue, and Jack be nimble . . . But she couldn't find Melissa.

She woke up sobbing, her pillow wet. What did it mean? Greg had suggested her dreams might be from something in her childhood. Something she had forgotten. Had she perhaps been traumatized by an automobile accident? Even one in a book or a movie? A car wreck where children were hurt—or a baby killed? Had she witnessed such a horror—and then been so shocked she had forced herself to forget it?

Well, if so, she had done a very complete job of it, because she certainly couldn't remember any such thing.

But there was one comfort. Horrible as the nightmare had been, now she could cling to Greg's theory that there *was* a rational explanation. She wasn't going insane.

Chapter 4

Charlie had proven himself to be a rare jewel of a plumber. Not only was the kitchen plumbing working, but all the mess of oily sand had been cleared away as well. If only the other stresses of the evening could be as easily scrubbed away, Debbie thought as she sat at the kitchen table, sipping her second cup of coffee the next morning. To her surprise, Byrl broke her unalterable rule of going straight to her computer as soon as she finished her granola. Instead, she poured herself another cup of coffee as well and settled in to talk. "Oooh, we had the most *marvelous* time last night." She stretched luxuriously. "Alex is an absolute business genius. Remember that *chic-looking* drive-in espresso place we saw at that rest stop outside Portland? Well, Alex owns that. He has a bunch of them. Besides, he's foreman of a big construction company." She gave a euphoric smile. "Money, brains, and muscles."

Debbie murmured an assent as she looked at Byrl. Byrl's plaid bathrobe was belted around her naturally lean form, which she stretched to full length with her bare feet on the chair across from her. "And how did you and Adonis fare?"

Debbie fingered the tassel on the zipper of the pale blue, lace-trimmed robe that hid her gently rounded curves—curves that stopped short of chubbiness but would never qualify as fashionably bony. "We didn't. Do me a favor. The next time you pick out a man to throw me at, please make sure first that he isn't married. OK?"

"*Married?* Are you sure? He doesn't *act* married." Byrl laughed and ran her fingers through her short brown, wash-and-wear styled hair. "So where is the inconvenient lady?"

Debbie shrugged. "I'm sure she'll be around soon."

"Good, then we can murder her, and he won't be married. See how simple it is when you put your mind to it?"

Debbie's answering grin showed her perfect white teeth. "You've been reading thrillers again. Why don't you go back to your power politics books?"

Byrl leaned forward. "Seriously, Deb. If he *considers* himself free, what difference does it make if he's separated or divorced or whatever? Besides, he isn't likely to attempt anything that would startle the horses in front of his daughter. So why be such an old silly about having a nice evening?"

Debbie didn't answer. She knew better than to try to argue morality—or anything else—with Byrl.

But then her cousin came in with one of those incisive remarks that showed how she always got to the heart of the matter with her interview subjects. "You *want* him to be off-limits, don't you, Deb? The only reason you haven't run back to Boise already is that you think he's *safe* because he's taken."

"No! That's not true." But she knew it was. She had been able to control her impulse to shudder whenever he touched her only by assuring herself that it meant no more than when her brother or father would offer a hand in assistance.

And, of course, that had to be the case. Dr. Gregory Masefield would never think of her in any serious way. Not if he really knew her. Now, Ryland Carlsburg—maybe he . . .

With such thoughts stinging her, Debbie did what she had always done. She took refuge in a creative project. The morning was gray and misty, perfect for spending indoors, anyway. She opened a box of fabric she had brought with her for just such an occasion and pulled out a bright print splashed with strawberries and daisies. She had been itching to turn that into cushions. She cut the print and a length of unbleached muslin into 16" squares. Then, sitting comfortably by the window overlooking the beach, she began stitching around each strawberry and daisy with tiny quilting stitches. When the outlining was completed she would slit the muslin backing and stuff each design with Polyfil to give it the puffy effect of trapunto quilting developed long ago by Italian artisans. As she worked, her needle made tiny metallic taps on her thimble and she could visualize the dinette of her little apartment . . . Cushions on the chairs, her collection of strawberry-patterned mugs hanging on one wall . . .

She would be fine there. Her new home would be safe. She didn't ask herself safe from what? Nor did she allow herself to consider the fact that to be truly safe she would have to be safe from herself—and from God.

The next three hours flew as quickly as Debbie's needle. When her stomach reminded her that it was lunchtime, she looked up to see a beach swept free of mists and washed in golden sunshine. The warmth pulled the vacationers from their rooms like an electromagnet. The beach was dotted with sunbathers, sand castle builders, model plane pilots, and kite fliers. Just outside her window on the Promenade children whizzed by on rollerblades and bicycles while dogs of every breed and description trotted contentedly on leashes. It was irresistible.

Grabbing a bright red apple and a chunk of tangy Tillamook cheese, Debbie headed out to the beach for lunch but turned around a few steps outside the door. It was never as warm as it looked at Seaside. She slipped on the yellow sweatshirt that matched the short skirt she was wearing and tried it again, remembering her sunglasses as well this time.

Now comfortable, she stood, wriggling her toes in the warm sand, crunching her apple and absorbing the exhilaration all around her: sparkling sun, cavorting children, winging kites. Especially the kites. Dozens of them filled the skyline the length of the beach: multicolored dragons—some that must be 50 feet long; rainbow-shaded windsocks with ruffling streamers; multitiered boxes . . . it looked like a regatta. A red and yellow exotic bird soared near, whistling in the wind. A small red triangle flew over, making a nervous fluttering sound.

But amid them all, one kite in particular took her attention. It was three diamonds tied parallel to each other—red, white, and blue—each with its own long tail. Two strings controlled it from the outer edges of the kites, and the pilot flew it in a spellbinding pattern of spins, rolls, and dives. It made an enormous whooshing sound as it swooped low over Debbie's head, then she held her hands to her eyes to watch it ascend again, dipping and darting across the sky until it flew right into the sun and she could look no more.

Then without warning, an erratic wind current dashed the proud craft to the sand where it lay in a dejected, crumpled heap. The aviator walked toward his fallen airship and a familiar voice called to Debbie, "Ah, just in time! Give me a hand, will you?"

Startled to realize that Gregory Masefield had been performing the exhibition that held her so spellbound, Debbie almost choked on her last bit of cheese. She coughed, then swallowed hard. "Sure. What do I do?"

Greg finished untangling the mass of crisscrossed strings. "Just hold the kites by the outer edge, about three feet off the ground."

She obeyed, feeling the tug of the wind on the kites. Greg backed away, straightening out the lines as he went. When he reached the handles he called, "OK, when you feel the wind take them, let go."

He pulled the lines taut. Debbie let go. The kite soared. "Oh!" She was enthralled. "What do you call it?" She walked to where Greg stood maneuvering the strings.

"Stunt kite. Just a small one. On a good day you'll see some 12 or 15 diamonds long. But this is enough for me."

"How does it work?"

"Watch. I pull one side to make it turn, then pull the other way for the opposite direction." The kite responded gracefully to the demonstration as he made two complete circles, then sent it looping back the other way. "You can only do a few loops in one direction, then you have to reverse for it to untwist."

Debbie looked at the length of cord that seemed to extend to the edge of the beach. "How far out is it?"

"Only about 300 feet."

"Only? That sounds like a lot."

"Not really. The world record is over 12 miles. Oops!" his attention went back to the kite as the red, white, and blue streak nose-dived toward the sand. Just before it crashed, he pulled it up once more into the bright sky. "We've got a good strong wind today so it's very maneuverable, but it requires constant attention. Want to try it?" he held the wooden handles out to her.

"I'd love to! Is it hard?"

"Not at all, just be firm. Follow through on your movements. And don't panic. Here, come stand in front of me."

He was wearing only cream corduroy shorts. His tanned skin gleamed in the sun. She hesitated. *Don't panic,* he said. Her heart pounded. Her palms were moist.

She didn't move, so he came to stand behind her. She could feel his sun-warmed body through her shirt. Part of her wanted to run. Part of her wanted to stay. She didn't do anything. "Now, put your hands over mine, and I'll give you the strings."

Do as the man says, Deb. You're only flying a kite. Her hands felt numb, but she reached up and put them on his. A glint of sun caught his wedding band. The sight steadied her. Yes, he was unavailable. He was safe. With a firm, no-nonsense attitude she took the wooden handles that held the strings. "Oh! Oooo." The kite tugged as if it would pull her up too.

"You've got your arms straight out. Pull them in as if you were driving a car." Greg had moved aside. A comfortable several feet from her. "Now, pull on the red handle and push forward with the blue, and you can loop it."

Debbie followed his instructions. "Oh! I did it!"

"Sure. Now pull the other way."

The kite looped obediently. "That's great! I never thought flying a kite could be so exciting."

She continued for several minutes, soaring with seagulls, reaching for clouds, then the kite made an enormous swoop as a strong rush of wind caught it. "Oh, no!" the beautiful craft lay in a crumpled heap on the sand. "Oh, I crashed it. I'm so sorry. Oh!" She ran forward, tears stinging her eyes. Broken. It was broken and mangled like the dolls and toys in her dreams always were. "I'm so sorry. I'll never do it again." A red streak spread over the tangled mass. She covered her face with her hands.

"Deborah, what's wrong?" Greg's hands grasped her shoulders and steadied her. "Take it easy. It's only a kite."

Only a kite? She looked at the pile of nylon and strings. The red streak was only a kite tail. Nothing more sinister. She fought to steady her breathing, to control her trembling. *It's only a kite. Only a kite.* She repeated it over and over, forcing herself to look at the innocuous jumble. She managed a strangled laugh. "Oh, I thought I'd broken it."

But Greg wouldn't be put off that easily. "It's more than that, isn't it? Like when Melissa got caught in the wave? Do you want to tell me what's troubling you? I might be able to help. I studied counseling before theology. I'd like to help."

She shook her head. "I don't know. I told you I have these dreams."

"And you had one now? About the kite?"

"Yes. Only it wasn't a kite. It was . . . I don't know exactly. Blood, I think. It think there's always blood."

"But you have no memory of an accident? Yourself or anyone else bleeding badly? Maybe one of the twins when you were taking care of them?"

"No." She put her hands back to her face. "No, no, no. I don't know. Nothing makes any sense. Maybe I am going crazy."

Greg took her hands and held them very firmly. "No,

Deborah. Listen to me. You very definitely are not crazy. Something has happened to you. Something that is causing you terrible pain. The need to identify and deal with pain is very, very normal. But you must deal with it. It won't just go away on its own."

"I want to. I really want to. I just don't know what to do." There seemed nothing more to say. "Where's Melissa?"

"Flying that dragon kite." He jerked his head in the direction of one of the bright streamers Debbie had noticed earlier.

"All by herself?"

"She's flying it by herself, yes. Dragon kites are weightless, they just find the wind and float on it—perfect for children. But she's not alone. She's with those older children from the cottage on the other side of yours. A nice family from Seattle."

Leaving Greg to straighten out the kite, Debbie followed in the direction he indicated. She couldn't decide whether being with Greg made her feel better or worse. The nightmares had been worse since she'd met him. She had certainly never before experienced them while awake. And yet his reassurances and offers of help were so comforting. How could she feel better and worse at the same time?

Was she doing the wrong thing to continue the friendship? He said whatever was bothering her had to be dealt with. But maybe not. She could always just go back to her sheltered, cocoon world. Well, not the same one she left, but she could build a new one. She didn't have to face this pain.

Just the thought of escaping made the awful waking nightmare recede. That was it. She would just say hi to Melissa and return to her sewing. But when she got to the end of the kite string, Melissa wasn't there. No one was. The handle had been buried deep in the wet sand, and the kite was flying itself. "Melissa!" she turned in alarm, scanning every direction. Where had the child gone? How long ago had she left? Nothing must happen to Melissa.

Debbie ran to a group of children building a sand castle. But the shining blond head wasn't one of those bent over the structure. Could she have gone into the water? Visions of the sprite dancing in the waves at Cannon Beach gave her chills. The mosquito buzz of a gasoline-powered airplane directed Debbie's attention to a crowd gathered by the dunes watching a man and boy fly the radio-operated toy.

Melissa stood with a group of children, clapping her hands as the plane whirred and looped saucily, chasing seagulls and kites with high-tech superiority. The 12-year-old boy holding the controls whooped his delight as the plane made a kamikaze dive at a flock of gulls pecking at a bag of spilled popcorn. The birds scattered with angry squawks.

Just as Debbie reached Melissa's side the plane, which was midway around a wide circle over the beach, wobbled in its circuit, stood on its tail, then plummeted in a crazy tailspin. "Careful!" The father grabbed the controls and rescued the craft, pulling it out of its dive just inches above the ground. "Now, look—" The plane flew around in an easy arc while the father lectured his son on the importance of holding the controls steady, turning the dials smoothly and—

Several watchers shrieked as the plane suddenly seemed to develop a mind of its own. It shot upward with a furious speed. Debbie grabbed Melissa's hand and pulled her backward. She didn't like the biting screech as the plane turned. Screaming at an attack pitch, it made a direct bomber dive at the head of the man bent over the controls.

He never looked up.

"Dad! Dad!" The boy sobbed over his father while the plane motor coughed and sputtered, half buried in the sand.

The little group who had a few minutes earlier been casually watching a father and son enjoying their hobby now froze with horror as a red trickle oozed from the man's temple and stained the pale sand. This was nothing that could be explained away as the streamer from a kite. This was real. But Debbie's thoughts were all for Melissa. She grabbed the child and turned from the scene. Melissa wasn't going to have nightmares over this if Debbie could help it. "Come on. Let's go find your daddy."

"What happened? Is the man hurt bad?"

"I don't know. But they'll take care of him. Would you like a Coke?" Melissa was slow to move. She wanted to see what was going on. But Debbie was determined to get her away from there. "Come on. Everything will be all right. Melissa, stop looking at that."

"But I want to know what happened."

To Debbie's relief Greg come jogging toward them from the far side of the dunes. What had he been doing over there? She thought he was out on the beach. "Look, there's your daddy." She tugged Melissa around.

"Daddy. A man's hurt. The plane hit him."

Greg took one look at the scene and scooped Melissa into his arms. "Let's take a look."

"Greg, no!" Debbie grabbed his arm. "Don't let her look. It's—it's serious."

"But she's already seen, hasn't she? What she wants now is to understand. Come on, Punkin. Tell me what happened."

Debbie couldn't believe it as Greg moved away, talking to his daughter, calmly answering her questions. Now everyone had come out of their initial shock. Someone was feeling for a pulse at the man's wrist, another bystander was halfway to the Promenade to call the medics, a young man with an authoritative voice directed the crowd to move back. A woman who appeared to be acquainted with the boy was comforting him. And everyone was discussing their version of what they'd seen: "Erratic little things. Hard to fly." "Silly to let a kid try it—they're adult toys." "Don't understand it. It couldn't have been affected that much by the wind."

Greg came back, still carrying Melissa. "We don't think there's much we can do to help here, so we're going to feed some hungry seals."

Melissa clapped her hands. "You'll come help us, won't you? They need lots to eat."

Debbie blinked. The child had witnessed a gruesome accident. Her father had deliberately taken her to where she could get a clear view of the bleeding man. They had talked about it. And now Melissa was fine. "I—I don't know."

Greg touched her arm. "Take your time. You've had a shock. Will you be all right if we go on, or would you rather we stay with you?"

"No, no. I'm fine. I just want to think. Alone. Really."

He nodded. "OK. If you're sure. We'll take the kites in, then go on to the aquarium. Join us when you feel ready."

Debbie turned back to the accident scene. The man hadn't moved. Was he . . . ? she couldn't bear to finish the thought. It was only a toy. Such fun. It all happened so fast. It wasn't possible that anything really serious could happen just like that.

The medics arrived and bore the man away on a stretcher. The woman followed with her arm around the boy. "What happened? Did you see it?" A familiar voice made Debbie turn. Ryland Carlsburg.

"Yes, I saw it—but I don't know what happened. The plane just went crazy and attacked him." She shook her head. "I know that sounds wild, but it's what it looked like . . ."

"You're trembling. Can I buy you a cup of coffee?"

Debbie looked at him blankly. "I don't know. I—"

"Allow me to rephrase that. Come along. You need a cup of coffee." He took her arm and led her to the sidewalk.

She didn't like his touch. But it seemed like too much work to resist.

After barely 20 minutes in Ryland's company, however, Debbie began revising her opinion of him as a sleazy playboy. Everything he did spoke of thoughtfulness and concern for her well-being. And her nerves responded on cue as her trembling stopped and the warm drink relaxed her.

To take her mind off the scene at the beach, Ryland chatted about his development company and his plans to bring new life and more tourist revenue to Seaside. "This is a special place, peaceful, relaxed, with incredible views in every direction. There should be facilities so more people can enjoy it. Environmental wackos accuse us of wanting to destroy the environment. But we wouldn't do such a thing. After all, it'd be killing the goose that laid the golden egg. Maximize, not destroy. That's my motto." He signaled the waitress to refill both their mugs.

"We'd likely have it done by now, but we had a tragic setback a couple of years ago—had a whiz of an attorney who had the wheels greased for all the permits—" He shook his head. "Killed in a car wreck. We had to start the process all over again." He took a sip of his coffee. "Well, now, have I thoroughly bored you? Enough to make you forget that unpleasant excitement?"

Debbie smiled. "I do feel better, but not because I'm bored. I'm interested in your plans. When do you start construction?"

"As soon as the committee approves our environmental impact statement, and a few other—well, technicalities. Come on, let me show you." He left money for the bill and got to his feet.

They walked back along the Prom to the site of the proposed hotel. Debbie smiled at Ryland's enthusiasm as he paced off the footage and described the ocean front restaurant, the ballroom, the pool and spa that he envisioned in each area. "Well, good luck. It sounds great."

"It will be great. If we can just build a fire under a few stick-in-the-mud types. But I expect approval any day now. We hope to be operational within a year. Matter of fact, some of our people are wining and dining some of the zoning council tonight. Very posh affair at a restaurant up the highway. How about coming with me? Salmon, crab, plenty of booze. Soft lights and a killer of a band. What time shall I pick you up?"

"No. No, thanks. I couldn't. I've, er . . . I'm busy tonight."

He gave her a penetrating look. "Pity. We could have had a very good time." He shrugged. "But then, if you can't, you can't. And there's always next time."

"Yeah. Sure. Thanks for the coffee." She turned toward the aquarium. "I have to go now. I promised to meet a friend."

"Right. Catch ya later." He strode off with a jaunty wave.

Debbie watched him go. Why did she feel attracted to him? She couldn't imagine wanting to spend an evening with plenty of booze and dim lights. And yet—there was something . . . She thought of Greg in comparison—putting aside for the moment the fact that Gregory Masefield was safely married, of course. She had far more respect for him. But that was part of the problem, wasn't it? Deep down she knew that any man as fine as Greg couldn't really like her. He was kind and thoughtful, always offering to help her— now. But if he really knew her—knew what she was like inside—he wouldn't want to have anything to do with her. Ryland Carlsburg wouldn't care.

Chapter 5

Debbie almost ran down the Promenade toward the huge, gray barn of a building that was the Seaside aquarium. She hoped Greg wouldn't be angry with her for keeping him waiting. *Take your time,* he had said, and he always seemed so patient. But he wouldn't have thought she'd be this long. Her father had always demanded punctuality, and she had tried very hard not to let him down. She always tried so hard to keep people satisfied, to meet their expectations. She hated it when those around her were unhappy. Especially since she always felt it was her fault when things went wrong. And then she would try to control it all. And then more would go wrong. And then it would be her fault.

She increased her speed and almost collided with a little boy just getting the feel of his rollerblades. All she would need would be for one more thing to go wrong today. She hurried into the aquarium.

Melissa and Greg were just emerging from the large, dark room where rows of brightly lit glass tanks displayed colorful sea life. "I'm so sorry. I didn't mean to take so long. I hope I haven't—"

"No problem." Greg's smile was relaxed. "We've just been looking at the exhibits."

"Daddy, can we show Miss Jensen the flowers?"

"Flowers?" In an aquarium? Debbie wondered.

"Sure, Punkin. I have to make a phone call. You show her your favorite fish, and I'll be back to help with the seals."

"You don't think they're too hungry to wait, do you?" Melissa glanced toward the long tank where the seals were barking and cavorting for the visitors who threw them bits of fish.

"They look fat and sassy to me. I'm sure they'll be fine."

Satisfied, Melissa grabbed Debbie's hand. "Come on, let me show you."

Debbie resisted the impulse to pull back from the small, soft hand holding hers. It felt so good. So warm and sweet. It was so reassuring to have a child offer her friendship and trust. She felt needed and valued. But that reliance was just what she wanted to pull back from. She concentrated on the tank Melissa pointed to. "Stars. See. Daddy says the bottom of the ocean is as beautiful as the sky at night. God decorated the top and bottom of the world just alike."

Debbie stood fascinated before the tank of starfish. Some with as many as 20 rays looked like giant orange sunflowers—some as big as two feet across. A mean-looking sculpin frowned at them through the glass, seeming to size them up for dinner. Then a great orange garibaldi fish swam by, its graceful fanlike fins undulating the water over delicate tangerine starfish lying splayed on the bottom.

"God did good, didn't He?" Melissa's enthusiasm made Debbie smile. Apparently the child's theologian father hadn't let a teaching opportunity go by. "Daddy said this shows how much God loves all life."

"I'm sure he's right." Debbie moved along to a row of high tanks displaying miniature marine life. She leaned forward for a closer look at the two-inch-long purple crabs.

"I can't see." Melissa tugged at her skirt.

"Oh, sorry." Well, there was nothing to do but to hold the child. Debbie couldn't understand her struggle over taking the small, warm body in her arms. The problem wasn't physical. Melissa was small for her age and feather-light. She smelled good, her skin was soft, her hair silky. Yet that was the very problem. As Melissa snuggled against her, the emotional pain was so sharp Debbie had to fight against crying out and pushing the child away. Instead she focused on the display before them. "Look, those are called pipefish. Can you tell which are the fish and which are the reed grasses?"

Melissa watched for a moment. "That one." She pointed. "He moved."

They continued around the room. Dozens of tiny silver gunnels lived in tenements of empty clam shells. Iridescent sea pens rippled like frilled feathers gracing the writing desk of an 18th-century lady. The transparent bodies of corn-stripe shrimp showed water running through their bodies like plastic tubing. Tiny volcanoes of barnacles adorned coral, peach, and mauve scallops. But best of all was the giant display of sea anemones filling one whole corner of the room.

"There! Flowers!" Melissa pointed. The mirror-backed tank was filled with an enchanted forest of white, coral, yellow, green, and red miniature trees topped with ruffled, feathery crowns.

"They look like flowers, but they're really animals—and very deadly to unsuspecting sea creatures that cross their path." Debbie jumped at the sound of Greg's voice. She had forgotten he would be returning. But she saw the truth of his statement as an attendant dropped a chunk of salmon into the mouth of one of the flowerlike creatures, and the innocent-looking petals immediately closed to devour it.

Melissa nodded with satisfaction. "Daddy says that shows all life is important."

Debbie laughed. "You've trained her well. A budding theologian at age six." Debbie turned toward the seals, wondering why Greg's precepts irritated her. Of course she agreed. She could hardly bring herself to pull weeds out of her garden in case they turned out to be flowers. So he needn't preach to her.

She let Melissa down and turned to the splashing, barking, diving seals who rocked on their platforms, shoved each other, and hit the water with disastrous results to the clothing of the visitors tossing pieces of fish to reward such antics.

Melissa squealed with delight each time one of the aquatic clowns stood on his tail and caught her morsel in his mouth, then clapped his flippers to thank her for the tasty tidbit. But her delight turned to dismay when she began getting soaked by all the activity.

Debbie took her to a private pool at the end of the room where a sign introduced a baby seal pup, born at the end of June. "See, he's almost a month old." Debbie pointed to the baby who observed them with huge, round, dark eyes. "You can't feed him. He's on a special diet."

"I want to pet him." Melissa stretched out her hand, but to no avail. After several moments she turned. "He looks kind of scared—like he doesn't want so many people staring at him. Maybe we better go."

They washed their hands at the sink provided for that purpose and emerged, blinking, into the late afternoon sunshine. "Will you come to our fire beach?" Melissa asked.

"Um—fire beach?" Debbie was at a loss.

"Beach fire," Greg prompted.

"We're going to have hot dogs and marshmallows and everything," Melissa urged.

"Well, I don't know." Debbie hesitated. She didn't really have any excuse. But it suddenly seemed as though it had been a very long day. "Maybe another time. I—"

"Please." Melissa turned her wide blue eyes up at her. The soft, round look held a special appeal.

"Give me an hour, and I can contribute a pan of brownies."

The cottage was cold and silent when Debbie entered it. A hastily scribbled note told her that Byrl was off with Dream Lover and Deb was not to wait up for her. Debbie shook her head and let the note fall back on the kitchen table. She didn't have time to worry about her cousin's escapades. She rushed to throw the promised brownies in the oven. They had been her brother's favorite, so she could make them with her eyes closed. She brushed her glossy black hair, then clambered into a pair of jeans and a heavy Aran sweater while the brownies baked. Greg and Melissa came to collect her just as the warm, chocolate scent from the oven signaled that they were done.

As they walked out onto the sand, the lowering sun was a glowing white globe, diffused by the thinnest veil of mist. It made the mica in the sand sparkle like glitter in a Christmas display and welcomed them to the beach by spreading a golden path at their feet. And it spun an aura of gold around Greg's head. Debbie pulled back with a sharp intake of breath, then steadied herself with the reminder that he was safely married. She had just come along as a companion for the child. They walked toward the more deserted end of the beach, the steady, soporific roar of the waves covering their silence.

Debbie pulled off her sneakers for easier walking. The sand, still warm from the afternoon's sun, shifted under her bare feet, feeling like deep-pile carpeting. They walked slowly, Melissa leading the way toward a special log she had scouted earlier with the neighbor children for the "fire beach." Debbie felt cold prickles as they neared the site of that afternoon's accident and was relieved when Melissa jogged ahead to a spot beyond.

As the sun sank closer to the wide, flat horizon, it changed from its silvery whiteness to a rich gold. Debbie turned to Greg to comment on the sunset, then stopped. Byrl had dubbed him Adonis, but the golden sunset turned him into Apollo. Debbie took a deep breath of the incredibly moist, fresh air with its unique salty, sea smell and told herself to think about Ryland.

Intermittently along the beach they passed clusters of holidayers sitting around crackling fires built in the shelter of drifted logs. The air took on a subtle smoky smell, a different brand of perfume from the astringent saltiness of earlier. Debbie was beginning to wonder if Melissa really knew where she was going. That special log she had seen could easily have been in the opposite direction. Or already claimed by other picnickers.

"Here it is!" Melissa's voice warbled across Debbie's doubts.

With considerable relief they flung down their load of blankets and baskets. "I was beginning to think you were putting us on about a special log, and what you really wanted was to walk to Astoria," Greg teased.

"But I was right, wasn't I?" Melissa gave her daddy a saucy grin.

"Indeed you were, Punkin." Greg knelt, laying out the kindling he had hauled to the site on his shoulder. "I don't think I've ever before seen a drift log with roots like these."

"They look like a haunted castle. That's why I chose it. You won't burn it, will you, Daddy?"

Greg scooped out handfuls of sand from beneath the log. "No, we won't actually burn the log much at all. It just shelters the fire."

Debbie turned to unpack the contents of the picnic basket. "It must be some incredible storm that brings these tree trunks up so far beyond the normal surf."

"They say the winter storms here are magnificent." The flame of Greg's flickering match caught and the kindling crackled. "I'd love to see one sometime."

Debbie wasn't so sure. All that unleashed power and fury sounded frightening. She busied herself preparing the hot dog buns. "Anyone not want melted cheese on theirs? Speak now or forever hold your peace."

"What are you doing?" Melissa asked.

"I'm going to wrap the buns in foil and warm them near the fire with the pork and beans."

"Oh. We always eat them cold."

Debbie made a face. "I think they're disgusting cold. Want to help?"

With meticulous concentration, Melissa followed her instructions for putting cheese slices on the buns and wrapping them in foil. "This looks good."

"It will be. You're a good helper. Come over someday and you can help me make chocolate chip cookies. I have a secret formula that I divulge only to my very best friends."

Melissa grinned from ear to ear. "Do you mean it? Honest?"

"Cross-cross applesauce." Debbie solemnly crossed her heart.

Melissa laughed and repeated the words. "That tickles my ears."

Debbie stuck a wiener on a stick and handed it to Greg. "Every man for himself."

Greg obediently roasted his hot dog to plump juiciness and popped it in one of the buns Melissa had prepared. They followed the sizzling cheese-and-bean-dogs with plump red/black Bing cherries, popping them into their mouths by the stems, then spitting the seeds into the fire. "It's the only way to eat cherries," Greg said. "Civilization takes all the fun out."

By the time the three of them had demolished Debbie's brownies, still warm and chewy from the oven, they were all lounging helplessly on the blanket, their backs against a sand dune, far too full to move. The beach was now dark. Only the flickering lights of other fires told them they were not on a deserted island. The glow of the flames shed a circle of gold on the threesome, enclosing them in warmth and shelter.

Melissa snuggled into the curve of her daddy's arm, put her head on his chest, and went to sleep like a kitten curled before the hearth. "I don't believe it," Debbie said. "She does run down."

"Sometimes it happens. And the nice thing is, once she's out, she's really out. She sleeps as hard as she plays."

Debbie sighed with the contentment that only a warm fire and a full stomach could produce after an active day. She started to shift to an easier position on the sand dune when she felt Greg's arm circling her shoulder. His hand clasped her arm. She rolled away. Then sat up. "I'm sorry. So sorry! I don't know what I've done, but—" Her heart pounded in her ears. Her palms were sweaty. "I—I came for Melissa's sake. That's all. I—I didn't mean anything."

Greg looked alarmed at her reaction. He carefully shifted Melissa to a more comfortable position on the blanket and sat up, moving away from Debbie in the process. "What is it? I didn't mean to frighten you."

"I—I—" Debbie swallowed and looked around. They were on the beach. Why had she thought she was enclosed in a car? She could have sworn she felt a steering wheel poking her ribs. Now she saw it was only the root of the old log. She tried to control her trembling, but her hands still shook. What was this? Greg was so safe. She had been so sure he was safe. She felt sick at her stomach. No man was safe. She should have known. Not even a well-known Christian leader. Especially not.

The flickering glow from the fire highlighted the strong bones of Greg's face, accenting his crisp, blond hair and deepening the intensity of his eyes. But the face she saw wasn't his. It was much younger, softer. The hair brown, shoulder length. The eyes confused, hurt. She put her hands over her eyes to shut out both faces. "Don't touch me. I didn't want that!"

"Debbie, I don't understand."

Greg's calmness contrasted with the frustrated, offended voice that rang in her mind. "Oh, Greg. It's you."

"Of course, who did you think it was?"

"I—I don't know. I—" She bit her lip.

"Debbie, what's the matter with you?"

"With me?" Suddenly she flared as she looked at the situation before her. "Nothing's wrong with *me*. I'm just not in the habit of being cuddled by married men."

"What? You couldn't possibly believe that. How—?"

"One." She pointed to the sleeping child. "Two." She pointed to his wedding ring. "Three, 'Mrs. Masefield.'"

Greg looked blank. "Mrs. Masefield?"

"That's what they said Sunday."

"Oh, of course." He hit his forehead with an open-palm gesture. "My mother. She's an organist—well-known in these parts. She played for the closing service of the conference, then went back to Portland." He sat for a moment staring into the fire. "Gayle was killed in a car wreck just over two years ago. She was a lawyer—had been in Salem for her biggest client—coming home in the middle of the night. Went to sleep at the wheel on the freeway."

They sat in silence for several moments as Debbie worked through the emotions this new information produced. Part of her was pleased that this man wasn't married. Part of her was terrified that the safety wall she thought had existed between them was wiped away. But most of all, her feelings were for Melissa. Debbie looked at her. She was so small, sleeping so soundly curled in the fetal position. Her features were so soft and innocent in the golden firelight. It took all Debbie's control to keep from diving across the blanket and scooping the child protectively into her arms.

The very thought of it produced such an aching void inside Debbie she wanted to stuff her fist down her throat to fill it. All the years she had spent raising her sister, trying to find fulfillment in the meticulous attention she gave to Angela, but never being able to quell the ache. Then having Angela go off and marry . . .

Here was another child: sweet, innocent, motherless. Here was someone who needed her nurturing. In that moment she felt as securely bonded to Melissa as if they were tied together with actual cords.

"Time to get Melissa to bed." Debbie jumped at the sound of Greg's voice. She had forgotten he was there. "Can you manage the picnic things so I can carry her?"

"Sure. No problem." No, the equipment was no problem. It was light. It was Debbie's heart that was heavy. Nurturing Melissa would mean building a relationship with

Melissa's father. A situation that was complicated by the fact that he seemed more than willing. And most complicating of all was the fact that part of Debbie was willing too.

But back in her room she looked at her reflection in her dressing table mirror. The deep blue eyes with the surprisingly long eyelashes and heavy, dark brows looked levelly at themselves. "How can you keep forgetting that you aren't what he thinks you are?" But what *was* she?

The problem wasn't what Greg thought. It was what *she* thought. And she didn't know.

Chapter 6

Debbie sat up in bed after only a few hours of sleep. She wasn't screaming or crying, but the ominous air of a bad dream hung in the room. She looked at the little white tablets on her nightstand. She could take one and sleep dreamlessly. Well, no, that wasn't exactly true. Dr. Hilde had explained that she would dream. She just wouldn't remember it when she woke up. That was what she had just done anyway, without the pill. And she didn't feel very good about it. She would almost rather face the terror than live with the sense that something nasty had happened. Something she couldn't remember.

She closed her eyes and a remembered face came at her from the dark corner of her room. The same face she had seen on the beach last night when Greg put his arm around her. "No. Go away. I don't want to think about you."

Debbie switched on her bedside lamp. The light fell on her Bible. Long ago she might have turned to its pages for comfort as her mother had taught her to do. Certainly she would have prayed. The long-forgotten memory of the comfort she had once known made her clutch her chest. But now she was cut off from all that.

Oh, she still believed. She still went to church regularly. She said the confession. She repeated—and believed—the Apostles' Creed. She even took Communion. And she knew it worked for everyone else. If Byrl would let her, she would gladly explain the plan of salvation to her cousin. And she fully believed Byrl would find a fulfillment that literary success, power politics, and a string of men hadn't brought her. Deborah Ann Jensen was the only one not worthy of pardon.

A thin gray dawn outside told her that actual sunrise was still a couple of hours away. It looked cold and damp out there, but the small cottage felt confining—as if it were holding in all her frustrations, pushing them in on her.

She pulled on a sweatshirt, then a jacket over the top of that as protection from the weather, and slipped out the back door. At first she walked at a brisk pace, outdistancing her problems and embracing the invigoration of being the only one on the whole beach at that hour. She had to share her world with no one but the seagulls.

Maybe that was the answer. Sharing her world with Greg, Melissa, even Ryland, produced nothing but confusion and frustration. Why not just escape into her design work and forget about it? Even as her mind formed the thought, she knew it was impractical—those people were here. And they wouldn't go away so simply. But for the moment the idea was so appealing she decided to grasp it and enjoy the release of not having to worry.

She breathed deeply of the moist, fresh air and jumped over the low balustrade of the Prom onto the soft sand. As she climbed a gently rounding dune growing with long, coarse grasses, she realized she was in the area of yesterday's accident. She shivered at the memory, wondering how the man was and hoping the shock hadn't been too terrible for his son.

Almost at the top of the dune, her foot struck something hard in the sand. Thinking it was probably a child's beach toy, she stooped to dig it out.

Debbie shook the sand off the flat, six-inch square plastic box and stared at it, wondering what she held. Then she remembered seeing it in the father's hand as he and his son bent over the controls of the plane. The horror of the moment returned to her. She instinctively ducked as if something were coming out of the sky at her and dropped the controls as if she had discovered a smoking gun.

Then she realized how silly she was being and picked it

up again. They would want it back. She could take it to the hospital or newspaper office or something—they would know who the man was.

She slipped the control into the pouch of her sweatshirt and went on over the dune toward the water. Although the windswept sand was clear of any ominous red stains, her mind was still on the accident. Then she realized that the control couldn't have been dropped by the father at the moment of the accident. It was on the far side of the dune, not where they had been flying the plane. She paused a moment and looked back at the scene. Yes, she was sure.

Well, someone else must have picked it up and carried it off—probably a child who soon lost interest in playing with the buttons and then buried it in the sand. What a fluke that she ever found it. Talk about a needle in a haystack. One of those things that could never have happened if she'd been looking for it.

She turned back once more to look at the site and discovered she was no longer alone on the beach. She waved as she recognized Ryland's windblown curls. "Hello. Are you a morning person too?"

"Not usually." He fell into stride beside her. "I had a lot on my mind this morning."

"Thinking about your project?"

He nodded. "Trying to think up new strings to pull to get it approved. How such pigheaded, blind fools can get elected to office—" He laughed and placed a hand casually on her shoulder. "But you'll straighten them all out when you're president, won't you? Are you thinking of running for an office next election?"

Debbie didn't know whether to laugh or scream in frustration. How could one offhand remark haunt a person for so long? And now she couldn't tell Ryland it was just something she had said to get rid of a drunk. He had been the drunk. She shook her head and sighed. "That was only intended as a witticism."

"Pity." He shrugged. "Land developers need all the powerful friends they can get—especially when they're of the beautiful female persuasion. I think I told you, we lost a most effective advocate in that area. Oh, well." They walked on together quietly, listening to the roar of the surf. "Are you sure you don't want to reconsider? There's a vacancy on the city council now."

"What?"

"Oh, haven't you seen today's papers? The man who died on the beach yesterday was a councilman."

"What? Died!" Debbie gasped. How could Ryland say that so calmly?

"He was dead on arrival at the hospital. That solid spruce plane crashing into his skull made quite an impact at the speed it was going. Bad luck that it hit his temple."

"Dead." She took in a deep gulp of air. "That means I saw a man die right before my eyes. It just doesn't seem possible . . ." Her hand brushed the front of her sweatshirt, and she remembered the little black box she was carrying. "Look what I found in the sand." She drew it out and held it with two fingers as if it were loaded. "It looks like equipment for that plane. Do you think it might be?"

Ryland took it. "Where did you find this?"

Debbie waved vaguely toward the sand dune. "Over there. Do you think they might want it?"

"Hmm, I suppose the family might. Shall I take care of it for you?"

"Please. I feel as if it were a murder weapon."

Ryland laughed as he stuck the control box in his pocket. "Oh, I don't think there's any suggestion of foul play."

"No, I didn't mean that. It's just that . . . Oh, I don't want to talk about it."

"Want to go home?"

She nodded.

He took her to her doorstep. "Will you be all right?"

Debbie forced a smile. "Of course. I'm just being overly dramatic. I don't deal well with death."

"No one does." He took her hand and squeezed it. "I'll call you later. Maybe a few days, though. I have to go to Salem."

She escaped into the cottage, but its coziness held no refuge from the horror she had witnessed the day before. Byrl sat at the breakfast table holding out *The Signal* with inch-high banner headlines: COUNCILMAN LARSEN DIES IN FREAK ACCIDENT ON SEASIDE BEACH.

Debbie took the paper with cold hands. "Civic leader Duane Larsen was pronounced dead on arrival at the Seaside hospital yesterday from injuries received when the model airplane he was flying went out of control . . ." The vivid picture in Debbie's mind replaced the printed words. She had no need to read an account of what happened, so she skimmed to the bottom of the column. "Larsen is survived by his wife Margaret, son Rick, 12, and daughter Megan, 7 . . ."

Debbie skipped to a companion article of interviews with local citizens. "He'll be sorely missed. Duane was one of our most valiant crusaders for public causes." "He will be long remembered for his fight against the casino-gambling forces seeking to get a foothold in our area." "Larsen's death leaves a vacuum that won't be easy to fill. The antigambling movement is leaderless for the time being."

Debbie crumpled the paper. It was so senseless. How could something like that happen in an ordered universe? No matter how distant her relationship might be, she did believe God existed. An all-powerful God who had permitted this to happen. How could He stand by and allow such things? She threw the paper to the floor. "I need to talk to Greg."

She found her neighbor still reading his morning paper. "How can it be?" Her voice was accusatory as she pointed to the lead story. "You're the theologian. Can you make sense out of such things? Do you have any answers?"

Greg looked up slowly. "None you haven't heard before, probably: That God doesn't cause evil, but He permits it because we are living in an imperfect world; that what looks like chaos here will look like perfect order in the next life when we see God's plan in total; that God can use even evil things to bring about His purposes." As he spoke he poured a cup of coffee and handed it to her.

Debbie cupped the mug with her fingers to warm them. "Yeah, I've heard it before. And I suppose it's all perfectly true. But it comes out sounding like a lot of pie-in-the-sky platitudes."

Greg didn't wince at her attack. He'd probably heard that before too. "I think one of the best approaches is to look at the other side. Why do so many wonderful things happen? Even to people who don't deserve them? For every child born deformed, look at how many are born beautiful and healthy; for every person killed in a freak accident, look at how many have narrow escapes; for every awful thing that happens to someone undeservedly, look at the number of good things that happen equally undeservedly.

"The answer is grace. God's unmerited favor to all His creation. It's the source of every good and wonderful thing that ever happens. That, of course, doesn't answer why evil and terrible things happen. That answer is much less pleasant, although no less true—"

Debbie nodded. "I know. Sin."

"Yep. At the very root of all unhappiness—although the person suffering from it may not be the sinner himself. The possibility of evil must exist for us to realize good; just as dark is necessary for us to understand light. Without evil in the universe we wouldn't have a choice. And God doesn't want to be served by puppets." Greg shook his head and laughed. "Whoa. Sorry, you didn't come over here for an instant theology degree. I'm afraid I get that way when I've been out of the classroom too long. Have I helped at all?"

"Yes, you have. Like you said, no easy answers. But plenty to think about instead of just reliving that scene on the beach. Thanks." She set her coffee mug down and stood up.

Greg walked her to the door. "Anytime. Maybe I should hang out a shingle: Gregory T. Masefield, Consulting Theologian. Wonder how much I could charge an hour?"

Debbie's little giggle was the first happy sound she'd made all morning. It changed the feeling of the air around her. Byrl was still at the breakfast table when Debbie returned to the cottage. "Well, you look considerably happier than you did half an hour ago. Decided to quit being fussy about outmoded things like marital status?"

"Oh, I haven't told you. He's not married after all. His wife died more than two years ago."

Byrl clapped her hands together. "See, what did I tell you? I honestly don't understand why you were so hung up about it. But since you were, I'm glad it's worked out. Wonder why he still wears his ring?"

"Because he loves her, of course. Perfect woman. Perfect relationship. You don't quit loving someone just because they aren't there anymore. And, of course, there's Melissa. I don't know, it just seems proper to keep his wedding ring on when he has a child."

"Proper! Oh, you funny thing, you. You really are frozen in the past. Don't you know the rules have changed? A meaningful relationship, that's what's important. Not a piece of paper some priest did voodoo over." Debbie started to protest, but Byrl went on, "Fortunately, Alex doesn't worry about such outmoded ideas. His suite at the Shalimar is gorgeous. And he's extended his stay for another two weeks. Then he wants me to move into his condo in Portland with him until his company starts some big construction project here. I had been thinking of going on down to San Francisco when our lease is up on the cottage, but now I don't know— he's a very tempting hunk."

Debbie didn't reply. It would be useless to try telling Byrl that Truth doesn't change just because society's ideas do. But it would be interesting to point out how outraged she'd be if a man referred to her as a tempting chick.

Byrl picked up her mug. "See you later, darling." She disappeared into her room to begin her day's work while Debbie attacked the breakfast dishes with verve. They had agreed that Byrl would pay the lion's share of the rent and Debbie would do the housekeeping, but she would have done it just the same no matter what the financial arrangements. Debbie never let a dirty dish stand on counter or in sink for more than 10 minutes. Nor did she ever leave a bed unmade or a floor unswept. And yet, she always wondered why an antiseptically clean house was never as satisfying as she thought it was going to be. Probably because she could never really get it clean enough. Just as she could never be good enough at anything.

She was just reaching for the can of Lysol when there was a knock at the door. Melissa stood there with an apron shaped like a teddy bear tied around her tiny waist. She held out a wooden spoon. "You said we could make cookies."

Debbie thought briefly of the soft sculpture she had hoped to finish that morning, then turned back to the little upturned face. "OK." She held the screen door open for Melissa. "Does your daddy know where you are?"

"Oh, sure. He said it was OK. Just so's I didn't disturb you. And if we bring him some cookies."

Debbie pulled a stool up to the counter for Melissa to stand on, then turned on the oven and got out the ingredients. "I'll measure things, and you dump them in the bowl, OK? Here, can you crack eggs?"

Melissa wound up with almost as much of the slippery egg white clinging to her fingers as in the bowl. While Melissa washed her hands, Debbie dug bits of shell out of the bowl and wondered if she should put in another egg to make up for what her little helper spilled. Then she decided this would likely be par for the procedure, so if they spilled an equal percentage of everything the measurements should come out right.

She leveled off a cup of white sugar with the side of her knife and handed it to Melissa. The child had successfully washed her hands, but the drying had been less thorough. Bits of the sweet white crystals stuck to her damp fingers, and she occupied herself with licking them while Melissa packed the brown sugar into a measuring cup with the back of a spoon. "Why are you doing it that way?" Melissa asked.

"To get an accurate measurement. Brown sugar is lumpy. It won't measure flat if you don't push it."

Melissa was delighted when the sugar plopped out in the bowl still holding the shape of the cup. "Oh, just like building sand castles with a bucket!"

"Yes, it is, isn't it?" Debbie smiled. This was perfect. The perfect mother-daughter activity. She had always tried to get Angie to work with her in the kitchen, but her sister was always too busy with parties and school activities.

"Did you make cookies with your mama when you were a little girl?" Melissa asked.

"No—" Debbie stopped. She had started to say that she never had. But maybe there had been a time. Before her mother got sick. Before everything went wrong. But it was so hard to remember. Had there been good times?

She seldom looked back. It was too painful. Whenever she tried, she always hit a wall of anger that was like bumping a hot stove.

"Tell me about it."

"Hm?" She jumped at Melissa's simple request.

"Tell me about when you were little."

"I don't remember much about when I was your age."

"OK. Tell me about when you were older. Did you go on picnics?"

Debbie could remember sitting in a circle with her friends, pulling sandwiches and apples out of brown paper. "Well, not exactly picnics. But I remember eating school lunches with my friends. They always had notes their mothers had tucked in with their tuna fish sandwiches. I never had a note because I made my own lunches. Then one day I had a note. 'I love you. Have a nice day.'"

Melissa clapped her sticky hands. "Oh, good. Did your mama sneak it in to surprise you?"

"No. I put it in myself."

Melissa's face fell. "Oo, that's sad."

"Is it? I thought I was very clever. No one ever knew."

Just then Melissa squealed and jerked her hand away from the counter. "Yuck! A bug. A nasty black one. Smash it."

Debbie looked at the insect ambling across the countertop. "Oh, no, that's a cricket. I never kill them." She scooped it into her hand, held it loosely, and released it out the door.

Melissa regarded her with amazement. "Why did you do that?"

"My mother said crickets were lucky. Besides, I don't like to kill things."

Next Melissa knocked a saltshaker into the flour canister and reached in to retrieve it. She emerged, shedding flour all over the kitchen at the very moment Greg stuck his head in the back door. "I just came over to check—" The cloud of flour caught him in the face as Melissa waved to her daddy. He exploded with a sneeze. Then he surveyed the mess on the kitchen counter and floor. "Melissa, I told you not to be a pest. That isn't necessary, Debbie."

"Depends on what you consider necessary. How else is she going to learn?" She suddenly felt defensive. Words rushed out to justify her actions. "That's how I learned, sitting on the counter and watching every move my mother made. Sometimes she'd see me doing something and ask, 'How'd you know to do that?' and I'd say, 'I've seen you do it.' . . ." Debbie's mouth fell open as she heard her own words. Was that true? Had she had a relationship like this with her mother before—before . . . ? She must have. Debbie had certainly learned her domestic skills somewhere.

"Well, if you're sure it's all right."

Debbie blinked. "Yeah. Sure. We're fine." With a swift

mood shift she gave him a playful shove toward the door. "Now you just go back to where you came from. I'll call if the pipes break, but this is my department."

Greg grinned and retreated. "Just so you don't forget that eating is my department."

"What's the secret formula?" Melissa asked when Debbie finished wiping the flour off the child's face and arms. "You said there was a secret formula."

"Wheat germ," Debbie replied in a stage whisper, taking a jar out of the refrigerator. "We use less flour than the recipe calls for and replace it with wheat germ. It makes the cookies extra chewy and good for you. But don't tell anybody, because nobody likes food that's supposed to be good for them." They giggled at the conspiracy.

In spite of the amount of chocolate chips and cookie dough they both snitched, they managed to produce a batch of tempting golden cookies, crisp on the outside, soft inside, and full of melted chocolate morsels. "Another secret is that it's very important not to overbake them. Take them out as soon as they're a light gold." Debbie placed the cookies in the pie pan her small assistant held. "There now, take these to your daddy. Be sure you eat them while they're still warm."

"Is that another secret?"

"No, everybody knows that. And drink milk with them."

Melissa nodded solemnly. "You're coming, too, aren't you?"

"You don't think I'd let you walk out of here alone with all the loot, do you?" But before either of them could make a getaway, Byrl entered, following her nose to the kitchen. Debbie grinned at her. "You wouldn't like them. It's a very old-fashioned recipe."

Byrl stuck her tongue out at her cousin and took a handful of cookies back to her desk.

In the Masefield kitchen Melissa carefully poured glasses

of milk while Debbie washed some strawberries she found in the refrigerator. Just before calling Greg from his study, Debbie ran out and picked a handful of the bright orange and yellow nasturtiums that grew by the side of the house and put them in a low pot in the center of the table.

Greg's face lit with delight when his daughter led him to the table. He devoured a cookie in two bites, then raised his glass in a salute. "To the domestic arts and the resident artists."

Debbie lowered her eyes. The nurturing pull she had felt the night before returned with force. She thought of making a home for these two people in front of her. Making them cozy and happy: Thanksgiving dinners, Christmas decorations, Fourth of July picnics—all the fun and details of daily living that made life rich and beautiful.

But of course she could never take Gayle Masefield's place. And the sooner she moved away from here the less torn she was going to be. Empty, maybe, but at least not torn. She wondered what kind of woman Ryland Carlsburg admired. He didn't deserve as much as Gregory Masefield. So maybe she could be good enough for him. Maybe she would find out when he returned from Salem.

". . . so you'd better go get a sweater." Debbie jumped. What was Greg saying to her?

"Sweater?"

"Didn't you hear a word we said? You nodded when Melissa asked if you'd come on a walk with us, so I thought we must be getting through."

"Sweater. Right." She jumped to her feet.

Chapter 7

It was a gloriously sunny day due to the cool wind that had blown all the early morning clouds away—or rather, blown them high overhead where wispy white puffs floated lazily against a bright backdrop and colorful, long-tailed kites dipped and soared with the seagulls. The ocean, which had been such an ethereal silver-blue the night before, was now an intense navy, hinting at its hidden depths while multiple rows of white lace frothed at its edge.

Long, thin blades of dark green beach grass bent in the breeze, and Debbie was glad for the soft red sweater she had pulled on over her denim skirt with the red and white gingham lining. She also enjoyed the comfort of having her hair tied back in a red bandanna under the straw hat she plopped on for sunburn protection.

They walked northward on white sand strewn with bits of broken shell. Pieces of crabs, clams, and sand dollars looked like bumps on dotted swiss fabric. Melissa ran this way and that, collecting a bouquet of seagull feathers while Debbie considered the man walking beside her. He moved with long, easy strides, both hands stuffed in his jeans pockets. She liked his off-white sweater with the well-worn leather patches on the elbows. He must have felt her survey, because he looked at her, his eyes crinkling at the corners, then held out his hand. She took it, squelching the little voice of caution in her head with a stern, *well, why not*? She desperately needed to sort things out. And she knew all too well that running away wouldn't accomplish anything. They walked on up the beach, swinging their arms in rhythm with their step.

A few hundred feet off shore a huge flock of birds was feeding, skimming just inches above the water, then diving for food and riding the waves before circling again for another course. Beyond the birds, several fishing trawlers were working the waters. "What are the seagulls feeding on?" Debbie asked after watching the birds for several minutes.

"Not seagulls—sooty shearwaters, actually—feeding on anchovies."

"Anchovies?" Debbie laughed. "I thought those were oily little things that are great on Caesar salad and awful on pizza."

"This is before they get to the cans, Landlubber."

"So the boats are fishing for anchovies?"

"To be used on Caesar salads but not on pizza?" He grinned at her. "Fact of the matter is, they're fishing for salmon. Anchovies are the primary food source in these waters for birds and fish. The salmon work on them from the bottom and the birds from the top. And just be glad you aren't an anchovy."

"With or without a pizza. Also not to be a salmon with the trawlers around."

"Chain of life. Part of the plan."

Debbie nodded. "Yeah. Pretty neat. Just so something like an oil slick doesn't come along and upset the applecart—or the fish basket."

"That's right. Man is part of the natural environment, too, which is a point a lot of environmentalists miss. But man has to be careful how he uses God's creation."

Debbie considered for a moment. "So where would you say a luxury hotel on the beach would fit into that? It would make more men—and women and children, of course—comfortable. Make it possible for them to enjoy the beauties of nature more."

"Would it? Or would it just allow the developers to make more money? Is there a lack of facilities here now?"

"Well, I don't know." She'd have to think about that.

"I don't think vast tracts of land should be sealed away from the public. And generally timber and wildlife management are good stewardship. But environmental issues are just like any other—they need balance. Man's needs should be considered along with everything else—like the timber worker with a family to feed. But we do have to remember that greed is part of man's nature, and that has to be kept in check too."

She nodded, thinking the topic closed as they walked on.

Then he said, "Gayle and I used to go around and around about this. You know she worked for Ryburg—trying to get Carlsburg's building permits."

Debbie was too surprised to reply. It had never crossed her mind that Gayle Masefield might have been the beautiful, brilliant lawyer who was greasing the wheels for Ryland. "She had been in Salem for *Ryburg* when she had her wreck?"

She hardly noticed Greg's nod as she considered the implications. Ryland had encouraged her to run for office so she could take *Gayle Masefield's* place? She was thinking so hard it was several moments before she realized she was staring at a flock of delicate brown and gray birds playing along the edge of the water. They ran in ahead of the waves on their sticklike feet, then followed the water back out again like children. Melissa instantly accepted their unspoken invitation to run with them, although the birds then moved a bit further up the beach.

Debbie smiled as she watched the child. "That's great. She doesn't seem to have any fears left over from falling at Cannon Beach."

"I'm so thankful about that. I was worried. She's had so many insecurities in her life, but she always seems to bounce right back."

He meant her mother's death, of course. Debbie was again overcome with a sense of compassion for the child.

She slipped her hand from Greg's and went out to join Melissa. Together they ran to keep ahead of the white foam as it swept up the beach, then turned to chase the retreating waves across the satiny sand, watching the water make little V shapes as it flowed over scattered pebbles.

Greg joined them, and Melissa turned to her daddy. "I want to find some seashells."

"Further up the beach we might. There are usually some good ones where the river comes in." Greg led the way. What with taking so much time playing and looking, their progress was slow, but when they neared the mouth of the Necanicum River Greg's prediction came true.

"Look, Daddy! A sand dollar. And it isn't even broken! Well, not very much," she added when she saw the chip on one side.

"That's OK. The design is perfect." Greg examined the round, flat shell with a five-petaled flower stamped on its smooth top. "Do you know the legend of the sand dollar?"

"I don't," Debbie replied. "But I'd love to hear it." She sank down on the warm, soft sand. "Any excuse to sit for a minute." They had been going slowly, but their progress was steady and the little town of Seaside and its populated beach was way behind them. Here there were no homes fronting the beach, just huge, grass-covered dunes.

Greg knelt between them. Melissa bent her head over the shell in her daddy's hand, watching closely as he pointed out each part. "This shell tells the life of Jesus. See the tiny star in the center? That's the Christmas star that guided the wise men to Bethlehem. The petals around it are a poinsettia, the Christmas flower." Melissa smiled and traced the pattern with one finger.

Greg turned the shell over. "But here the flower is the Easter lily. These five wounds," he pointed to tiny holes in the shell, "are the wounds Christ suffered from nails and Roman spear." Melissa put a hesitant finger to each hole.

"And then inside," Greg snapped the shell in two and

shook five small white triangles out into his hand. "Are five white doves waiting to spread goodwill and peace."

"Oh!" Melissa cried with surprise and took the pieces into her own hand.

"And, so, as the poem says, 'This simple little symbol, / Christ left for you and me, / to help us spread His gospel / through all eternity.'"

Melissa turned to search the sands, but Debbie didn't move. "Is that what you teach your theology majors?"

"More or less, yes. It's the heart of the matter." Their eyes held. Suddenly theological issues seemed very far away. "Deborah—"

"Daddy!"

Greg shrugged and offered his hand to help Debbie to her feet as Melissa ran to show them her treasure—a tiny white shell shaped like a volcano. Greg pulled a plastic bag from his pocket, and Melissa dropped the shell in it.

"And I thought I was the one who was always prepared. I'm impressed." Debbie laughed.

"Experience." He turned back to Melissa. "Sometimes you can even find periwinkles here. And there should be some unbroken crab shells."

"Oh, good." Debbie took Melissa's hand. "Let's try to find some nice ones. If we get enough I'll do a collage—on burlap with tiny seed pearls . . . and stitch a seaweed effect with brown yarn . . . and lots of French knots . . ." The wall hanging took shape in Debbie's mind as she spoke. "Maybe we could find a piece of driftwood to hang it from too."

They all hunted at the edge of the water, up and down the beach, bent almost at 45-degree angles so as not to miss any treasures. "Here's a new kind!" Melissa ran to show them the hinged halves of a razor clam.

Debbie looked at the prize for a moment, thinking. "I've got it. We can make angels. We'll dress little dolls in long lace dresses and use these for wings. You can put them on your Christmas tree."

Melissa jumped with excitement and dashed off to search for more. Greg shook his head. "You're amazing. You never run out of ideas, do you?"

"It's a disease. One idea breeds about six more. And I'm constantly frustrated because I can never keep up with all my projects."

"It's no wonder you're excited about your career as a designer."

"Well—that's a mixed blessing. I won't really be able to develop my own projects when I'm working eight hours a day on other people's things." Besides, the point of it all was to create a warm, beautiful atmosphere for people she loved. Not just to make things for money, but she didn't try to explain.

When their beachcombing bag was full, they turned their backs to the ocean and crossed the broad expanse of sand toward land. Just before they reached the dunes Debbie spotted a bright gold Frisbee abandoned by some child, half buried in the sand. "Catch!" She flung it at Greg.

He stretched out his arm almost lazily and caught it with easy grace. Then with a barely perceptible motion he tossed it to Melissa, who squealed and dashed at it with both hands. "Very good!" he called as she caught it. "Now send it to Debbie."

The golden platter spun round and round the three-cornered circle with Melissa giggling every time she dropped it or sent it too far afield for Debbie to catch. But Melissa soon tired of the game and went off to dig in the sand.

Debbie's attention was distracted momentarily by a white seagull gliding against the bright blue sky. "It's yours!" Debbie turned to Greg's shout just in time to see the Frisbee coming right at her. She screamed and covered her head with both arms. Feeling incredibly silly as the missile fell to the sand at her feet, she picked it up and laughed. "That's why I never could play baseball in grade school—I was always afraid of the silly ball." She didn't want to admit that for an instant she had thought of a model airplane zeroing in on her.

"And I'll bet they never could teach you to keep your eye on the ball, either."

"You're right. Do you have any idea how impossible that makes playing tennis?" Determined to get even, she hurled the Frisbee back at him with a forceful fling of her arm. The results were embarrassingly disappointing. "Why does it wobble?"

He picked up the disc and tossed it back to her effortlessly. "Use more strength in your throw—the wind makes it harder."

Not wanting to admit that that was exactly what she thought she had done, Debbie gritted her teeth and tried again. Wobble. Plop.

Greg picked it up with a grin that Debbie found maddening. "You're using your whole arm. Just flip your wrist. Here, like this—" He gave her the Frisbee, then, still holding her hand, guided the throw. The Frisbee flew into a gentle arc and settled on a clump of beach grass.

But neither of them saw it land. Greg increased the pressure on her shoulder to turn her to him. The melting she felt had nothing to do with the warmth of the sun.

Until his lips touched hers. "Shawn! No!" Her fingernails scraped the side of his face.

Greg jumped back, his hand to his cheek.

Debbie looked at him in horror at what she had done. "Oh, I'm sorry. So sorry. I—" She turned away, clutching her stomach.

"Debbie." Greg's voice was calm, gentle. He took a step toward her but made no move to touch her. "Who is Shawn?"

"A boy I knew years ago."

"A boyfriend?"

She nodded, her eyes on the ground. "We dated all through high school. He was Young Life president. He . . . I . . .

He . . ." She shook her head. It was impossible. She wasn't even sure what she was trying to say.

"He went too far?"

"It should never have happened. He was this big Christian leader. He knew how I felt—what I believed . . ."

Greg sat down on the nearest dune. "And I'm a Christian leader. And you can't trust me either?"

Debbie sat down several feet from him and began doodling in the sand.

"Do you want to talk about it?"

"I don't know. Maybe, but there isn't really anything more to say."

"Have you had other boyfriends since then?"

"No. That was just when Mother got sick." She paused to think. "As a matter of fact, it was the very day I found out she had cancer. I never had time for dating after that."

"You took over your mother's place in the family?"

She nodded. "Pretty much as soon as we knew she was sick. Then completely after she died. Someone had to take care of Angie and Andy, of course. And I'd always been good at cooking and things like that."

"And then college?"

"Yeah. I'd been planning to go away. I'd picked out a college in Boston. But then that was impossible, of course. So I went to Boise State."

"And did brilliantly."

She shrugged. "I got A's. But they didn't really mean much. I still felt—empty."

They were quiet for a while. "Where's Shawn now?"

"I don't know, and I don't care." The bitterness in her voice was a shock. "I never saw him after that night. There wouldn't have been time even if I'd wanted to. And of course I didn't want to." She jumped to her feet and started back toward town.

She had gone on this walk hoping to sort out her feelings, maybe even come to terms with her relationship with

Greg and Melissa. Not only had she failed miserably, but the situation was now far more confused than before. Perhaps her initial instincts had been right—hiding *was* the only safe plan.

She was some distance down the beach when Greg caught up to her. "Debbie, will you give me a chance to prove that it doesn't have to be like that? Some men can be trusted."

Yes, she thought. By other women. Some women merit trustworthy men. She shook her head and started to answer him when she caught a glimpse of Melissa tossing a feather into the breeze and chasing it. The ache to nurture overwhelmed all her other fears. And these two were a package deal. Did that mean she must lose Melissa too?

Chapter 8

"Letters for you," Byrl called from the kitchen when Debbie closed the front door with a more dispirited thud than she had intended.

"Letters? As in more than one?"

Byrl tossed two white rectangles to her. Debbie stuffed all the turmoil of the afternoon deep down inside her, as she had long ago learned to do, and concentrated on the familiar world conjured up at the sight of her father's and sister's handwriting. Byrl sat across the table reading her fan mail, sorting it in two stacks—love and hate. Debbie's cry of dismay was so sudden in the quiet room that Byrl got a letter in the wrong stack. Someone was going to get a very puzzling form reply to the letter they wrote to Byrl Coffman.

Debbie held the letter away from her, blinking. "Angie. She's going to have a baby."

"When?"

"Mid-March."

"That's *great*. But you don't sound very excited. I would have thought you'd be over the moon for your baby sister to have a baby. You're going to be an aunt."

"Yeah. Sure. Of course I'm happy for her. If she's happy."

"Well, does she *sound* happy? What does the letter say?"

Debbie looked at the sheet of floral paper she was still holding at arms' length. "Yeah. She sounds happy. Delirious, actually."

"Well then?"

"I don't know. I mean, what if something goes wrong?"

"Oh, no! Not the fussbudget routine again. I remember the big Thanksgiving dinner—one of the few times I actually made it to a family bash. Angela cut her finger. You made me take her to the *emergency room,* for goodness' sake!" Byrl shook her head in exasperation.

"We were cooking poultry. You have to be very careful about salmonella."

"If you were going to freak out, the least you could have done would have been to take her *yourself.*"

"I had the dinner—"

"Spare me." Byrl held up her hand. "All I'm saying is that you always overprotected her."

"It was my job to take care of her. And I did too. But now . . . I hope she's ready for this. She and Ron haven't been married very long."

"Well, if she doesn't want it, she doesn't have to have it. There *are* alternatives."

Debbie pretended she didn't hear Byrl as she turned to her other letter. Her father and Leonora were back from their honeymoon. He said getting a new wife and a grandchild in less than a year made him feel at least 10 years younger. And he suspected he would need to be to cope with it all.

Her father didn't sound worried about Angela. But then he wouldn't, would he? He was a man. Besides, their dad had never worried about any of them. He had put in 10-hour days at the store, then come home for supper and the newspaper. Worrying had been Debbie's department. It was a good thing nothing had happened to her. She couldn't imagine what would have happened to any of them if it had.

But was there something that had almost happened? She remembered that she was supposed to ask her father about that when he got home. Had she had a near-drowning or witnessed an automobile accident or something like that? But that seemed silly. She would remember if she had. Greg had just been grasping at straws—pulling stuff from his counseling books to make her feel better. Nothing to bother Dad about.

Byrl dropped her last envelope on the table. "What's for dinner?"

"Aren't you going out with Alex?"

"He said he might be around later. That's fine with me. No strings, you know."

Debbie opened the refrigerator and stared into it blankly. All the leftovers stared back at her from their tidy, airtight wrappings. She couldn't even think what she was supposed to be doing. Should she be with Angie? If Byrl would drive her into Portland, she could get a flight to Boise—

"You're wasting electricity. Environmentally unfriendly."

"Huh?" Debbie started at Byrl's remark. "Oh, yeah. Um, how about cheese and crackers?"

Alex arrived in time to join them for the last of their snack. "Well, good news. The move to Portland may be off. Just had a talk with the head honcho. He tells me Ryburg may break ground on its project by the end of the month."

"Ryburg?" Debbie put her cracker down. "You mean you work for Ryland Carlsburg?" First Gayle, now Alex. Did Ryland control everybody?

"That's it. The espresso shops are a good investment, but I like more action. I'm Carlsburg's right-hand man. Whole right arm if the truth were known."

"Does that mean he got final approval for his project?"

"He called from Salem this afternoon. Says it's as good as in the bag. Seems the last barrier has been removed."

"Well, I guess I'm glad." Debbie hesitated. "I mean, I'm glad for Ryland and for you and for all the people who will enjoy the hotel. But I hate to think of these cottages being torn down. This really feels like home."

"Hey, can't let sentiment stand in the way of progress. Think of what it'll do for the local economy." Alex got to his feet.

"Don't wait up." Byrl shot Debbie a glance over her shoulder as she led the way out the door.

For once Debbie didn't feel like sewing when the kitchen was back in its pristine condition. So she curled up in her favorite chair in the living room and picked up the novel she was reading. She had been overwhelmed last winter when she'd seen *The Potting Shed* on TV. Now she finally had a chance to read more of Graham Greene's work, but she was having trouble getting into *The Power and the Glory*. Already, though, she had been impressed by how easily the characters spoke of matters of faith with no trite phrases, so she pushed on.

It wasn't long before the story of the priest who "wondered whether he was even fit for hell" captured her imagination. Greene's characters took life before her as living, breathing people. She sat reading, her feet curled under her, for two hours. When she looked up she was amazed to see that it was dark outside. The chill in the room made her shiver. She started to jump up to turn on more lights, then almost fell, gasping with pain. She couldn't straighten her legs out. Hours spent walking in the sand, followed by a long period of sitting in a restricted position in a cold room had combined to produce a case of severe muscle cramps.

She rubbed the backs of her legs until the friction warmed them and she could move. There was only one thing to do for this. The cottages shared a hot tub and sauna in a small building in the backyard. A massage from the steamy hot, whirling water was exactly what she needed. She twisted her long hair into a loose top knot and climbed, stiffly, into her powder blue swimming suit.

She wrapped herself in a long white, terry robe and hurried with awkward movements across the lawn to the spa room. After flicking on the soft gold ceiling lights and turning on the motor to send the water in the small pool surging in pulsating circles, she dropped her robe on a lounge chair and lowered her aching muscles into the steaming water.

"Ahhh." Her whole body turned into a jellyfish as she relaxed with the penetrating warmth and massaging motion. She slid forward until her shoulders and head were supported by the edge of the tub. She let herself drift . . .

"Don't you realize that could be dangerous?" A reproving voice penetrated her euphoria.

She opened her eyes and blinked to focus them. "Greg. What are you doing here?"

"I saw you come in and I came to talk to you. It's a good thing I did. If you'd slipped over sideways, I could have found you floating facedown."

Debbie caught her breath at the look of concern on his face. "Oh, I don't think so. I was just relaxing—sore muscles from all that exercise today." Then she realized he was wearing a robe.

"Debbie, I won't if you don't want me to. But would you mind if I joined you in the pool—on my own side?"

She looked around. No one would hear her if she screamed. He had asked her to trust him. Could she do it? He was waiting, standing just inside the door, his black flannel robe firmly belted. If she said no, he would simply turn and go. And she could return to her relaxation.

"It's OK. Come on in."

"You're sure?"

"I'm sure."

Only then did he toss his robe onto the deck chair and cross the redwood floor to the hot tub. "You said you wanted to talk to me?" she asked when he was settled into the steamy water.

"To apologize really. For today at the beach. I didn't realize I was rushing things so."

"Oh, please don't apologize. I know I was being very silly."

"No. You aren't silly at all. Your honest reactions are very normal."

Normal? He had used that word on her reactions before. "Well, I guess that depends on your idea of normal. Byrl thinks I should be locked up."

She had meant it as a joke. But he didn't take it that way. "Listen to me, Deborah. You're at a Fourth of July parade. A firecracker goes off. The man standing next to you pulls you to the ground and throws himself on top of you. What would you do?"

"I'd call the cops. Have him up for assault."

"Right. But if you knew he was a combat veteran who'd been trained to protect civilians in case of attack, what would you think?"

"That he was well trained and I'd be glad of his company if there were any terrorists around."

"Yes, you see. For a trained combat veteran his reaction to that firecracker was laudable—and normal for him."

"Oh, I see. Shawn was my war."

"That's right. And any protective actions you take in triggering circumstances are, for you, normal."

She nodded.

"The question is, do you want to stay shell-shocked? Or will you let me help you recover?"

Debbie felt the situation was just as clear as the clouds of steam fogging the room. She could see no way through. "Where's Melissa?"

"Asleep."

"You left her alone? What if she wakens?"

"Left her a note."

"She can read?"

"Drew a picture. We have a code. But it's time I got back to her." He stood, water running from his black swimming trunks. "Think about what I said."

Debbie shivered as the cold night air from the open door hit her. But it was nothing to the chill of her own thoughts. *But he doesn't know. He doesn't know . . .* Each rotation of the whirlpool seemed to increase her agitation. It had relaxed her muscles, but her mind was tight as a high tension wire. Could she open up to Greg? And what was there really to tell if she did? She knew there was no rational explanation to her reactions, even if he thought differently. He said he could help. He'd been a counselor. But he didn't know she'd already had counseling.

Chapter 9

Hearing a male voice on the telephone the next morning was like touching a fence and discovering it was electric. Then Debbie almost cried with relief. It was Ryland. "Oh, are you back? I saw Alex. He said things were going well for you."

"Yes, they are going well. But I won't be back for a few days yet. I'm calling from Salem to be sure you haven't forgotten me. I want to take you out to celebrate when I return."

"That sounds like fun. It's nice to hear from you. Very nice."

And Debbie continued to tell herself that the empty spot inside her was relief as she saw neither Greg nor Melissa during the next few days. The turmoil she had known settled into a dull ache—a constant throb that she was all too accustomed to coping with. She knew Greg was developing a study manual to accompany his newest book, *Created in His Image*. And sometimes as she worked at her designs in the living room she would for a moment think the clackity-clack of Byrl's computer was Greg's long fingers on the keyboard.

Debbie! her mind shouted. *You can't trust him. And you don't care anyway.*

You are obviously sick, she told her mind. *So don't shout at me about your problems!*

And even as she bickered with herself, the one thing she couldn't deny was that her arms ached to hold Melissa. She could almost imagine that Melissa was her child. Melissa could almost fill the void inside her. And yet she had no right to try to mother Melissa.

She got up with a sigh and turned to the day's tasks. She had discovered years ago when she began keeping house that the inevitabilities of life were not, as the saying went, death and taxes. They were laundry and dishes. She smiled as she remembered the motto her mother had hung over the washing machine at home: *This is the day the Lord hath made. Rejoice and do laundry in it.*

Debbie continued in the same vein of thought a short time later as she sorted clothes into machines at the Laundromat. She remembered reading a story once about an old woman in some war-torn country in the Orient. The fields and offices and all the places of men's employment had been destroyed. All the men who were not soldiers were left in idle despair. But the grandmother who must busy herself to scrape together a few bits of food for the hungry children in her care was the lucky one. She still had purpose in her life. Right then, Debbie had realized that the fact that a woman's work was never done could be her salvation rather than a curse.

And so it had been for her these past six years. Salvation and refuge. Now she had to find another sanctuary. And at least for the moment, her simple tasks provided that for her today. When she returned to the cottage, her arms filled with piles of satisfyingly clean clothes and linens, she was feeling much better. The only problem was that the stacks were so high that she couldn't see the back steps as she started up. She had no more than told herself to be careful than she almost fell headlong over an object on the top step.

When the object began to cry, she dumped her carefully folded laundry in a heap and gathered the child into her arms. "Melissa, darling, I'm so sorry. I didn't see you there. Did I step on you? Are you hurt?"

Melissa was more frightened than hurt. And disappointed that her attempt to surprise Debbie had gone so awry. "Well, I am surprised. But you should have cried out sooner." Debbie began restacking the scattered laundry. "Where have you been? I haven't see you for days."

Melissa shrugged. "Home. Daddy said we shouldn't bother you."

"He's right. You shouldn't. But the thing is, you aren't a bother. Want to make some more cookies or something?"

Melissa shook her head, dug in the pocket of her little blue skirt, and held out a handful of shiny copper pennies mixed with a few nickels and dimes. "Take me shopping." She looked over her shoulder to make sure she wasn't being overheard. "Daddy's birthday is next week. I want to 'sprise him."

"I'd love to go shopping." Debbie held the door open with her foot, her arms once again full of refolded laundry. "But what did you tell your father about being gone?"

"Um . . . well . . . I told him you'd invited me." Melissa stared hard at the kitchen floor. "But if you *do* invite me, then it won't be a lie—just foreknowledge."

Debbie laughed. "Your father is going to regret teaching you theology." She shook her head. "Well, for the sake of your spiritual condition, I guess I'd better issue a formal invitation. Just a minute, I'll get my purse."

This was the perfect solution to her dilemma. She could help Melissa but avoid Greg. Help the child while avoiding the discomfort of being close to the father. If this outing worked, perhaps it could set a pattern for the remaining weeks here.

In a few minutes they were headed down the boardwalk, Debbie practically jogging to keep up with the skipping Melissa. "Any idea what your daddy would like?"

"Yes. We saw it last week. He said it made him think of that verse about beagles—he likes it a lot."

Debbie scanned her repertoire of Bible verses. She'd gone to Sunday School all her life, but she was certain she'd never heard a verse about beagles. Jezebel being thrown to the dogs, maybe? Hardly hopeful as a favorite verse.

Melissa came to a stop before the window of a little gift shop near the top of Broadway. "See, there it is."

"Oh," Debbie broke into a smile of recognition. "They shall mount up with wings as *eagles.*"

"Yep. That's what I said."

The shopkeeper took the small porcelain eagle from the window so they could admire the fine craftsmanship of its delicately painted feathers and piercing eyes. Debbie especially liked the way the artist depicted the strength of the great bird even while working on such a small scale. Melissa dug in her pocket and produced the handful of coins. "Do I have enough?"

Debbie, standing behind her, held up her own billfold and nodded to the clerk. He grinned and solemnly counted Melissa's pennies. "I think that will just about do it." Then while Melissa examined the display of clown figurines along the far wall, Debbie handed him the remainder. She was surprised at the amount of change she received. The shopkeeper saw her confusion. "No sales tax in Oregon."

"Oh, of course. It's such a surprise to have things really cost what they're marked."

The shoppers went next to the little stores in Sand Dollar Square. At the Magic Flute toy shop it was hard to say which of them was the more delighted by the Kate Greenaway paper dolls, *The Secret Garden* book illustrated by Tasha Tudor and the tiny paper cottages that folded out to become stage sets for *The Three Little Pigs, Goldilocks and the Three Bears,* and *Little Red Riding Hood.* Debbie wished she could buy them all for Melissa. These were exactly the things she would hope to surround her own child with.

The unbidden thought was followed by a chill. She turned abruptly. "Come on, Melissa. Let's go to the kite shop."

Melissa clapped her hands. "Oh, goody. That's where Daddy and me got our kites."

But today the thing that took Melissa's eye was the bright silver puff balloons floating near the ceiling. "Which one do you like best?"

Melissa considered the dancing display of flowers, animals, and toys. First she pointed to a star, then a flower, then shook her head. "No, the Little Mermaid."

"Oh, that's a good choice." Debbie handed the clerk some money. "Here, let me tie it on your wrist." Before leaving the square they stopped at the Honey Bear Ice Cream Shop for strawberry ice-cream cones, then continued on downtown happily licking their cones as the sun glistened on the silver Ariel above Melissa's head. The street was alive with tourists enjoying the unlimited browsing opportunities of saltwater taffy shops, arcades, beachwear shops, antiques shops . . .

In the display of a lavender-painted store with antique lace curtains at the window Debbie spotted something she always watched for when she had an opportunity to poke around in specialty shops: a strawberry-patterned mug. This one was purple with a comic snail, wearing a strawberry for a hat. "See," she pointed it out to Melissa. "I collect mugs like that. I'm going to buy it. Then whenever I look at it I'll think of you and our shopping trip today."

"Would you let me buy it for you so you'd think of me too?" Debbie swung around in surprise at the masculine voice.

The combination of not realizing Greg was so close and not thinking about the ice-cream cone in her hand resulted in disaster to the front of his shirt. "Oh, I'm so sorry!" Then her contrition turned to giggles. It was several moments before she could control herself. "Let that teach you a lesson about sneaking up on people."

Greg watched ruefully as the sweet, pink mass slid down the front of his shirt and plopped to the sidewalk at his feet. As he pulled his handkerchief out to wipe up his shirt, a passing dog devoured the ice cream. Then Melissa bent to feed him the remainder of hers.

"I really am terribly sorry," Debbie tried again, but the effect of her apology was spoiled by the fact that she was still shaking with the effort of stifling her giggles.

"I can tell. You're heartbroken." Greg grinned. "No problem. I'm wash and wear."

"How did you find us? I didn't think you'd leave your computer for hours yet."

"I finished a chapter. I always allow myself a minicelebration when I do that. And since the metropolis is all of one street, I figured my chances of finding you were pretty good." He led the way into the shop. "And now that you've made the day truly memorable you'll have to let me buy you that mug. Let's see . . . a snail wearing a strawberry in memory of when Greg wore a strawberry ice-cream cone—it sort of works."

But this wasn't the idea at all. She had come out with Melissa to avoid Greg. Now all her disordered emotions erupted again. She'd been in a slightly hysterical state all day. The urge to giggle almost overwhelmed her. She didn't dare argue with him over the purchase. The most dismaying fact of all was the realization of how delighted she was with his company. After that night at the whirlpool she had determined to insulate herself from him. But the fact that he could so easily breach her hastily erected barriers showed how flimsy they were. There was nothing to do but make the best of it now, but she knew she would pay the price of painful regret later.

"Where were you going next?" Greg asked.

"The Christmas store!" Melissa jumped and clapped her hands. So they went down a small side street to a big old house converted into a year-round wonderland.

They were met at the door by the blond proprietress. "Take her around back." She looked at Melissa and pointed to the walk around the side of the building.

There they discovered a series of child-high windows. Debbie bent to Melissa's height to gaze at a perfect Santa's workshop. Half-finished toys covered the bench, teddy bears rode a teeter-totter, and a long, long list flowed onto the floor from Santa's desk. Under the decorated tree a toy train ran around a snow-blanketed village while tiny skaters glided on a mirror pond. All three pressed their noses to the windows, enthralled by the enchanted miniature world.

When they tore themselves away and went inside the shop, they found each room decorated in a different theme: a Victorian room, a circus room, a sugarplum room—complete with a tiny pink fairy dancing to her *Nutcracker* music. But Melissa's immediate favorite was the teddy bear room. There were bears at school—one reading a Paddington Bear book— a William Shakesbear, tiny bears, big bears, bears with curly hair, bears with straight hair, soft bears, prickly bears . . . "A prickly teddy bear?" Debbie frowned in disbelief.

Greg shrugged. "Bears are like people. They have their bad days too."

On the ceiling a circus of trapeze artist bears performed on the high wire. In front of the fireplace Douglas Bearbanks lounged beside a tea table with diminutive china in a teddy bear pattern. But of them all, Melissa loved the teddy bear wearing red flannel pajamas the most.

While her companions bent over *The Teddy Bear Catalog*, Debbie pulled out her compact and lipstick to make some minor repairs after eating her ice-cream cone—part of her ice-cream cone, at least. Melissa looked up. "Oh, you even have strawberries on that."

"Oh, my compact? Yes. This is really special." She bent down to show Melissa in detail. "This is silver, and see how the strawberries were molded in the metal before they were painted."

Melissa ran her finger over the shiny case. "Where did you get it?"

"I bought it in an antique shop. But not for myself. I gave it to my mother for Christmas one year."

"And now she's given it back to you."

"Well, I guess you could say that." Debbie dropped it back in her purse. "Anyway, it's the most special thing in my strawberry collection."

"I want to collect something too."

"That's a good idea. What would you like?"

"Teddy bears." Melissa gazed around the room, her eyes shining. "I already have two, so that's sort of a collection, isn't it?"

"It's a good start. And you have your teddy bear apron."

"Yes, I do!" The thought seemed to make her very happy. Debbie suggested that she choose something now for the official opening of her collection.

Since the pajama-clad bear was too expensive, Melissa chose a soft little three-inch brown bear that she could hold tightly in her hand.

They all three emerged onto the street with their eyes shining from having briefly experienced childhood. "You know," Debbie said, "the Cheshire Cat told Alice that once a child leaves Wonderland she can never go back. But it's not true."

Greg didn't reply. He just gave her a long, inscrutable look. When Debbie was beginning to feel uncomfortable with the silence he said, "Since I, er, interrupted your ice-cream cone, how about some tea?"

She nodded. Tea sounded good, but she really wanted to grab Melissa and disappear back into the teddy bear wonderland. Why did they have to return to the outside world at all?

They walked down the sidewalk between boxes of blue and yellow potted flowers on one side and storefronts trimmed with hanging baskets of deep red and purple fuchsia on the other. After crossing the bridge over the river they turned in under the striped canopy of a small shop and sat at a table spread with a brown and white gingham cloth, a vase of black-eyed Susans brightening the center.

Greg brought them steaming pots of Earl Grey tea—with lots of milk in Melissa's—and plates of crisp, rich shortbread and warm bran muffins with butter and marmalade. "Paddington Bear *loves* marmalade, but Winnie-the-Pooh eats honey when he gets a rumbly in his tumbly," Melissa informed them as she spread marmalade on her muffin.

"Oh, I'm so glad you're collecting bears. Every time I see one I promise to think of you." But instead of the smile Debbie expected her words to produce, Melissa looked as though she could burst into tears. "And I'll send you one too." That was all she could promise.

As they sipped their tea, Debbie looked across the room where shelves of gourmet food items and imported cookware lined the shelves. "I wonder if they have such a thing as a cozy for a single cup of tea? It seems like every time I pour a cup I get interrupted, and it's cold when I get back. If I just had a cozy to pop over it—"

"Couldn't you make one?"

She blinked. Such an obvious solution. Why hadn't she done that long ago? "Of course I could!" She dug in her purse for pencil and paper and began making a quick sketch. "There." She held it out a minute later. "I could do a whole set—a giant strawberry cozy to cover the pot, smaller ones for individual cups, and a hot pad for serving."

"That's brilliant. You could do a strawberry-patterned tea towel too."

"And an apron," Melissa added.

Debbie sketched more ideas to match their suggestions. "Wow, I could have a whole line." She added a ladybug climbing up the side of one berry and a tiny mouse tucked under the leaf of another. "I think I'll call it Melissa's Strawberry Patch."

"Then put a teddy bear in it."

Debbie reached for her cup as the ideas continued to flow. She took a sip, then set it down quickly. "Oh, see! It's stone cold. That happens every time."

They were all laughing when Greg offered his hand to help her slide across the bench she was sitting on. Debbie came up in one smooth motion, forgetting about the open purse beside her. It fell with a crash, the contents spreading under bench, table, and chairs. All three of them dropped to their hands and knees, scrambling to retrieve the scattered items. In a moment everything was back together and they were on their way.

"Any more shopping to do?" Greg asked.

"Not really. But let's just take a minute to go in that shop across the street."

"Something special there?"

"Very. Ever see any Cybis porcelain?" Greg looked blank. "Well, you're going to. Come on."

Debbie led them slowly by the windows displaying exquisitely crafted porcelain figurines, then stepped through the doorway and stood quietly inside the store that more closely resembled an art gallery.

"May I help you?" the proprietor asked from the back.

"No thank you." Melissa smiled. "We've just come to worship." They laughed at her obvious overstatement. And yet, nothing but such words as reverence, adoration, and awe could describe the feelings such matchless beauty stirred in her. Not worship of the objects themselves, but of the Creator who inspired the holiness of beauty.

"Cybis is America's oldest porcelain art studio," she told Greg in a voice just above a whisper. "Someday I'm going to own one. But I'm not sure I could ever decide which one."

They stood for some time gazing at the pieces from the English royalty series—Richard the Lionheart; his wife, Berengaria; his mother, Eleanor of Aquitaine—admiring the artistry of their ornate robes, the strength and beauty of their features.

"Here's Cinderella!" Melissa stuck her nose against the glass covering a low case.

"Yes, and look—that's Sleeping Beauty, and there's Rapunzel, and Alice in Wonderland." Debbie knelt beside her to point them out.

When she stood again Greg was looking intently at a

grouping labeled Adoration. "They came to worship too." Radiant angels knelt before the newborn Christ child. "They really are special. The flowing draperies remind me of Botticelli."

Debbie's thrill at his astuteness produced a tightening in her throat and a burning at the back of her eyes. At that moment she regretted the barriers between them more sharply than ever before. She managed a trembly smile. "You're amazing. Cybis has been compared to Botticelli—especially his *Birth of Venus.*" She pointed to a figurine reminiscent of the painting. A delicate figure poised on a shell with a gentle breeze blowing through her long golden hair and softly flowing draperies.

The shop owner approached. "The Cybis factory was begun in 1940. Boleslaw Cybis and his wife came to America from Poland to paint a ceiling for the New York Exhibition. When the war started they couldn't get home, so they opened a studio here."

He picked up a figure and ran his finger over it lovingly. "The satiny texture is achieved by grinding the clay so fine. They use a combination of American clays. No ash as there would be in bone china."

Debbie sensed that this connoisseur could go on for quite a while. And Melissa was showing definite tendencies toward restlessness. "Thank you so much." She moved toward the door. And again she vowed, "Someday."

A quiet moment over a cup of tea, the wonders of Christmas, the beauties of Cybis . . . As they walked home in the fresh evening salt air Debbie felt as light as the silver balloon floating gently above Melissa's head, reflecting the soft colors of the sun setting over the Pacific Ocean. They walked so slowly that at times they hardly appeared to be moving. Even Melissa seemed hushed by the gentleness of the beauty around them. Debbie had begun the outing with ideas of avoiding further entanglement with Greg. She had failed miserably to reach that goal. And yet she felt as if she had won.

The sunset came subtly, in delicately diffused shades of grays, mauves, and muted corals—a cotton candy world. Greg held out his hand. At that moment none of the old warning bells could hold her back. She placed her hand in his and smiled at the strength of his clasp.

They paused at the railing of the Promenade. "See the clouds on Tillamook Head?" Greg nodded toward the great green mountain projecting into the ocean at the south end of the curving beach. "Do you know why there are always clouds up there, even when it's clear and sunny on the beach?"

Debbie looked at the frothy white topping that hung on the mountains like angel hair on a Christmas tree and awaited a scientific explanation about vaporization of spray hitting the rocks and condensation at the cooler elevation. But she was surprised. "Cloud giants live up there. It's their job to hold onto the clouds."

Melissa clapped and giggled. "Do they hold fairy princesses captive?"

"Hmmm, I don't know. Guess we'll have to hike over there someday and find out. If there are any captives, maybe we can rescue them."

Melissa danced ahead of them along the walk, then stopped to look out over the water. "I think there's a boat out there, Daddy. Can I look in the scope?" Melissa stood on tiptoe before one of the telescopes mounted along the Promenade, trying to peer in.

Greg fished in his pocket for some change and brought out an assortment of pennies, nickels, and quarters, but no dimes. "Let me." Debbie swung her shoulder bag forward and began digging in its depths. "The fact that these things operate on a dime gives you some idea how old they are." She produced a silver coin.

Greg helped focus the lens, and Melissa narrated the scene before her. But Debbie continued digging in her purse. Billfold, notebook, lipstick . . . Something seemed to be missing. Only she couldn't figure out what it was. Deciding it must be her imagination she snapped the bag shut.

They were well on up the Prom when it hit her. Her compact. She stopped and began digging once more through her bag. "What's the matter? Lose something?" Greg turned back to her.

"My compact. It must have rolled clear under the bench when I dumped my purse at the tea shop. Rats! They're closed now too. I guess I'll just have to call them in the morning. My mother and I used to love to poke around in antique shops together. I gave that to her the last Christmas ..." She bit her lip.

"Don't worry. I'm sure it'll be safe. If we didn't see it down there on our hands and knees, it's doubtful anyone else will notice it."

Debbie nodded, and they turned again toward home. Melissa clung tightly to Debbie's hand, dragging her feet slower and slower. "Melissa's almost asleep on her feet. My mother always said shopping was the most tiring work in the world. Although I'm not sure you could call what we did real shopping."

"Want me to carry you, Punkin?" Greg bent to his daughter.

Melissa shook her head and clung to Debbie with both hands. Debbie nodded. "I'll carry you."

Melissa nestled in her arms, the little blond head snuggling on Debbie's shoulder. "She's going to get heavy," Greg warned.

"It's OK. It isn't far."

Quietly, so only Debbie could hear, Greg said, "She seems to have a mother fixation. She didn't get enough mothering when Gayle was here. Now she's really lost. I do my best, but—" He shook his head.

A hollowness in his voice told Debbie that Melissa wasn't the only one who missed the dynamic woman who was gone from their lives.

At Greg's cottage Debbie laid Melissa on her bed and carefully removed her shoes so as not to rouse her. She untied the silver balloon and let it float up to the ceiling, then pulled the soft quilt up to the tiny, pointed chin. She brushed the fine, pale hair back and bent to kiss the smooth forehead. After a moment's lingering gaze she pulled herself away.

She was startled to find Greg standing just outside the open door. "Would you come on a hike with us Saturday? I'd like to hide behind my daughter and say she needs you, but I'd be less than honest if I didn't admit that I do too."

The vision of the sleeping child was still bright in Debbie's mind. Now she turned to the strong, yet gently quiet man beside her. They were both so vulnerable in the pain they had suffered. Why did everything have to take her by the throat? It was so inconvenient not to be able to talk at a time like this.

"Hike?" she got out, hoping he wouldn't notice how strangled her voice sounded.

"We're going to check out those cloud giants on the top of Tillamook Head. Remember?"

Indeed she did. "I'll come armed," she said and sped away before Greg could offer to walk her over to her cottage. Try as she might, she couldn't find any armor he couldn't penetrate.

Chapter 10

The dream came softly, yet with great clarity. She was alone by the beach, sitting on a rock surveying a scene of intense beauty. The sand spread out an unearthly white, and the breakers rolled in bluest splendor before her. She slid lightly from the rock and strolled up the beach, her heart exulting in all she saw. She ached with the desire to share the moment. To share it with someone who was as special to her heart as the scene was to her eyes.

She woke, gasping for air through her constricted throat. Then the dream flashed before her, as vividly as she had dreamed it. Stark desolation washed over her. Could one die of emptiness? This dream of aching beauty was far worse than her nightmares of brokenness and violence. The anguish much greater as the scene of remembered beauty became one of abandonment. Bleak and barren.

And then, through the fog of despair, she thought of Greg.

Greg. He was the person she could share all the goodness and beauty of the world with. Greg.

Engulfed by a great sense of peace, rightness, and completeness, Debbie slept.

The dream was still with her when Saturday arrived and they started up the forest trail over the mountain. Lush foliage arched overhead to a blue-tinted cathedral ceiling. Sun fell in gold-mottled pools on the fern-and-moss-covered forest floor. Tiny sounds of birds, chipmunks, and beetles came to Debbie above the crash of the distant surf breaking against the rocks at the base of the cliff. Every breath filled her lungs with refreshing, woodsy air. Even though the ascending trail was steep and rocky, Debbie's feet barely touched the ground. The newness and wonder of her discovery floated to her on a magic carpet. She was in love.

Greg was her Someone. Someone to share life's beautiful moments. But what about the not-so-beautiful? What about the outright ugly? The ugly that filled more than moments. Would Greg share that too? Did she want him to? Could she let him?

She turned to look at him, just a few feet below her on the trail, his long legs striding up the path as if it were level, his golden hair reflecting glints of leaf-filtered sunlight, his clear blue eyes quietly surveying all around him. How would those eyes look at her if he knew? She shook her head firmly. *No. Just deny it. The pain would go away. For a while.*

She ached to be able to tell him what he meant to her. To tell him the good parts and bury the bad. She knew that if she put her hand to her chest she would feel the lump that was forming there from the dammed-up words. But perhaps he sensed them in part because he didn't speak when he reached her side. He just slid his arm around her waist and guided her gently on up the trail. And she let him do it. *Bury the bad,* she repeated to herself. That had always been her answer. There was no reason she couldn't continue with it. She would enjoy her day and worry about the consequences later.

But could she? Could she keep her fears bottled up? Could she keep Greg from guessing how she felt and thereby doubling the potential problems? Could she enjoy the day in such confinement? Well, she would have to, wouldn't she? There was no alternative. And Deborah Jensen had always managed to do what had to be done.

Melissa, water sprite turned wood nymph, danced up the trail ahead of them, her little voice joining those of the woodland creatures in the high, clear air.

"Don't get too far ahead of us, Punkin." But Greg's warning was unnecessary. Around a bend in the trail they found her, squatting stock-still before a dead stump. It was upright, but red and soft with decay, encrusted with moss and lichen, numerous small plants and ferns growing out of it. One side was hollowed out like a grotto.

"It's like a little house," Melissa whispered, her eyes shining.

Debbie dropped to her knees beside the child. "That's exactly what it is. It's a little house for bugs and tiny animals. I wouldn't be surprised of a little mouse or maybe a very small bunny lived in there. See that soft green moss in the back? That's probably his bedroom. And the toadstool is his table."

"But where is he now?"

"At the office, of course," Greg joined in.

"Oh, Daddy!" Melissa giggled and frolicked on up the trail.

Greg extended his hand to help Debbie to her feet. She brushed the decayed wood chips from her knees with her left hand, unwilling to remove her other from his grasp. A little further up the trail a clump of shamrocks grew green and bright over a mound beside the path. "Makes you think they would be complete with leprechauns and pots of gold, doesn't it?"

But Greg's reply showed how far his mind had strayed from the fantasy scene before them. "Debbie, what do you think of the idea that it's the quality of the mothering that counts, not the quantity?"

The question took her by complete surprise. She stopped for a moment and looked at him. His face was inscrutable, but she could only assume he was looking for compliance with Gayle's philosophy. The brilliant, beautiful wife who had balanced career and mothering so successfully that husband, child, and client still found her irreplaceable two years later. She felt like the heroine of *Rebecca*—finding red silk *R*'s embroidered on all the linens as constant reminders of the departed, adored wife. The question was like one of those fakey tests school guidance counselors gave.

You could always see how you were supposed to answer them to get the scores you wanted.

She took a deep breath. Well, there were some things you couldn't keep hidden forever. She might as well give him an honest answer. "I've always thought it was a convenient cop-out for people who would rather be doing something else. There can't be much quality if you're not there. Every child deserves to come home from school to find someone baking cookies for them once in awhile. You have to be there to do that."

"But that's not possible for some people."

"No. But those aren't the ones who try to justify their choices, are they? Besides, I thought we were discussing my idea of an ideal world—not the state of the economy." She hadn't meant her reply to sound so defensive. She strode on up the trail wondering why she had reacted in such a prickly manner. She slowed her steps, allowing him to catch up to her. "Sorry. I didn't mean to be so harsh. The thing is—childhood is so precious—every moment of a child's life. I just feel very sorry for mothers who miss it—especially those who choose to."

"Surely you'd feel sorrier for those who don't have a choice?"

"No. One regrets bad choices more than anything else." The forest silence closed in on them.

"But if that's how you feel," he sounded confused, "why—"

"Daddy, Daddy! It's a dragon!"

Melissa didn't sound frightened, but the alarming words sent them hurrying to her side. They laughed when they saw the dragon: a fallen log with snags of hanging wood forming teeth above a red tongue from a decomposing branch. Fluted lichens grew the length of its back, making effective scales.

"Well, of course the cloud giants would keep dragons. He's probably their favorite pet." Debbie looked at the woods growing like layer upon layer of green lace, mush-rooms and ferns tangling with the exposed roots of trees and bushes, moss covering everything like a bright green terry cloth towel. "It's easy to believe this forest is enchanted, but now we know the cloud giants are friendly. Nothing evil could live in such a beautiful place."

"That's right!" Melissa's voice held a note of relief that revealed just the tiniest concern for what they might encounter.

They crossed a corduroy bridge made of hewn branches placed side by side to cover a potential mudhole. Even in early August the ground was spongy from moisture in places. "No wonder it's so lush," Debbie said.

But Greg didn't reply. It was obvious he was deep in thought. She could almost hear the wheels of his mind turning. "Debbie, I don't understand—"

"The lighthouse!"

Debbie didn't turn to Melissa's shout. She sensed Greg wanted to say something to her. And she wanted to hear it. But he shook his head. "Later." Then he sighed. "And to think I was worried that she'd get too tired on the hike."

They came out to the clearing beside the trail where Tillamook Rock Lighthouse stood offshore. "I wish we could go *there!*" Melissa cried.

"Next to impossible." Greg shook his head. "I don't think anyone goes there now. They haven't used it since the '50s."

"When was it built?" Debbie asked.

"About a hundred years ago. I've read that, according to lighthouse keepers' logs, storms would sometimes throw large rocks through the lights and walls. Fish would be thrown more than a hundred feet into the air and onto the decks of the lighthouse. Can you imagine being out there at a time like that?"

Debbie shuddered. "I'm not sure I can even imagine being out there on a calm day." She surveyed the white foam spewing over the rock, nearly a hundred feet above sea level. "God would have had to create someone very specific for that job."

Greg shook his head. "No more so for that one than for any other. Every job has someone just right for it. But not everyone tries to find that special niche." He was quiet for so long Debbie thought he was through and wondered how she should reply to that. Then he added, almost as if to himself, "Sometimes people rush ahead on their own. Then they have to wait for Him to pick up the pieces. That can take awhile."

Debbie started to shiver but hid it as a shrug. She wasn't sure this was a comfortable conversation. "I wonder. How do you know what's right?" And how do you get back on track when you've derailed? she wanted to ask but didn't.

Greg started on up the trail, walking slowly. "I suppose the best answer I can give you is time. The Holy Spirit never rushes anyone. He has all the time in the world—after all—He made it." He paused and grinned. "But seriously, if you feel a sense of being pushed and hurried, it's doubtful that it's from God. A very wise man who's in heaven now taught me that—after I'd rushed ahead." He took a deep breath. "We always mess up when we take command of the reins—or steering wheel—or whatever."

Debbie held her breath, wishing he would go on. If he would tell her about the mistake he made once, maybe she could understand him better. But he was silent.

They reached the crest of the Head and started down the other side. "Melissa, don't run!" Debbie shouted as she heard the sound of little feet padding too quickly on the soft earth. "Please, don't run!"

Her pleas were answered with a giggle that sounded almost like one of the tiny, high-pitched bird chirps from the trees around them.

"Melissa." Her father's voice commanded with force, but no harshness. "Sit down and wait until you can see me."

"OK, Daddy."

Around two twists of the trail they found her perched on a mossy stump looking exactly like a small elf in her green shirt. Debbie and Greg sat beside her leaning against the stump. Debbie stretched out her sneaker-shod feet and sighed. "Uh-oh, I think this was a mistake. I didn't know sitting down was going to feel so good. I might not get started again for a while."

"Take your time. There's no hurry."

His words made her think of their earlier conversation. "You never rush people, either, do you?"

He looked at her with that special warm smile of his that came from his eyes rather than from his lips. "Try not to." Then he added. "But sometimes I'm afraid I'm a slow learner."

Even Melissa was quiet for a long time. Debbie felt an almost overpowering urge to lay her head on Greg's shoulder and go to sleep. Maybe she would dream again. And this time he would be there with her. But she didn't trust her dreams. It was better to stay awake while the reality offered all she could ask for. Later she would take her chances on dreams.

"Ooo, there's a bug on your hand!" Melissa drew back.

Debbie looked down at a large red, black-spotted ladybug crawling toward her wrist. She held her hand out toward a fern. "Ladybug, ladybug, fly away home." With a sharp puff of breath she blew the bug onto the plant.

"Are ladybugs lucky like crickets?" Melissa asked.

"Sure. They eat nasty bugs like aphids." Melissa gave a satisfied nod. Debbie was glad she didn't ask for more of the rhyme. *Your house is on fire and your children will burn* never seemed like a suitable nursery rhyme. She looked around. "This is such a beautiful little vale. I'd like to put a glass dome over it and take it home like a giant terrarium."

Greg pushed himself to his feet. "We'd better move before rigor mortis sets in. Tired, Punkin?" Melissa nodded. "Up you go, then." He tossed her effortlessly up on his shoulders. She folded her arms around his head like a hat.

He smiled at Debbie as she scrambled to her feet. "Are you all right?"

"Sure, I'm fine. But if I'd said, 'no,' would you have offered me a ride too?"

"Well, it might slow us down a bit. But I'd do my best."

Debbie laughed and scampered on down the hill, refreshed after the rest. Here the trail was carpeted with minuscule pinecones and bordered with mushrooms that were smooth on top and wonderfully fluted underneath like square dancers in ruffly petticoats. "Is it much farther?" she asked.

"Not much." Greg pointed to a clearing before them where she could see the dark form of rocks in the blue water. "That's Ecola State Park, trail's end—maybe a quarter of a mile."

"Ecola. Sounds like an Indian name."

"It is. Means whale or big fish. Part of our Lewis and Clark heritage. They had a salt works at Seaside and heard about a big fish that washed ashore over here. Captain Clark and Sacajawea and some of the others came across Tillamook Head to see if they could buy blubber."

"You mean *this* is part of the Lewis and Clark trail too?" Debbie looked down at the path under her feet. "Did they get their blubber?"

"You do expect a fellow to be up on his history, don't you?"

"Well, you're the teacher. How does he expect us to learn, huh, Melissa?"

"Was the whale dead, Daddy?"

"Yes. Probably killed by a storm. It was winter. And yes, they got their blubber. As I remember it, the whale had already been apportioned among the Tillamook Indian villages, but they were able to buy blubber and whale oil."

"Are you sure you're a theologian and not a historian?" As Debbie walked on, she tried to put herself in the place of Sacajawea, trying to feel the forest floor through animal skin moccasins, trying to imagine the weight of a papoose on her back. She stopped. How did she know that, she wondered?

Then she realized, the pictures of Sacajawea in her Idaho history books always showed the Indian women with an infant strapped to her back. "Did she really do all this with a baby?"

"Incredible, isn't it? But her husband was member of the party, so I suppose it seemed natural for her."

"Now I remember." Debbie's most recent reading of Northwest history had been in junior high, so it was rather vague. "He was a French Canadian who went along as interpreter. He won Sacajawea in a poker game or something, didn't he? And then married her."

Greg nodded. "She was only a child when she went hunting with her Shoshone people and was stolen by another tribe, then sold as a slave."

"What an amazing life!"

"But didn't she ever get to see her mama or daddy again?" the little voice from atop Greg's shoulders sounded very worried.

"I don't know if she ever saw her parents again, Punkin. But when Lewis and Clark were going through Shoshone country they needed to buy horses and supplies. The negotiations weren't going so well until Sacajawea met their chief. He was her brother."

"And needless to say, they got their horses." Debbie finished the story.

A few minutes later they emerged from the winding forest path to the radiant sight of Indian Beach at the foot of the cliff below them. A small, secluded beach with dazzles of gold sunlight dancing on waves that rushed up to the sand. Huge black, gothic rock structures stood defiantly in the ocean like the remains of an ancient civilization, white foam whirling against their sides.

"Want down?" Greg asked Melissa, but she shook her head, so she finished the trek triumphantly on her father's shoulders, like a maharani riding an elephant at the head of Hannibal's march.

They left the forest behind them and walked out onto

the flat, grassy knoll high above the ocean. Debbie was thrilled by the beauty of the scene until a nerve-rasping noise chilled her. It took her a moment to realize that it was the sound of a gasoline-powered model plane. Before she could stop her reflex, she threw her arms over her head and ducked. Then laughed nervously at her own foolishness.

"That accident still getting to you?" Greg joined her, watching the plane soar, its three-foot wingspan outsizing the many birds who made their home in the park.

"Like the combat veteran who dives to the ground when a firecracker goes off? I don't really think so. I just have hyperactive reflexes. But I feel as if we should warn those boys how dangerous those things can be." Three teenage boys shared turns at the controls.

A few moments later an argument broke out between two of them. "Don't ever do that! It's rotten sportsmanship and unsafe!" the long-haired blond shouted.

His companion, in a bright red shirt, laughed. *"Unsafe?"*

"To the plane. Want to crash it in the ocean?"

The third boy took the control from his protesting friend. "Here, if you're going to punch him, let me have this. You'll both crash the thing."

"Never mind, I'll bring it in." The red-shirted one produced his own control. He proceeded to bring the plane in on a smooth glide.

But the safe landing didn't pacify the long-haired youth. "Now look. When you want to fly the thing, ask for the control. If you get smart again with your own override, I'll smash it on the rocks. And your thick skull too!"

"Are they going to fight, Daddy?" The little voice was a reminder of the unsuitability of the scene for a child, so they left the hobbyists to battle it out and followed the trail along the edge of the cliff to the sunny park dotted with groups of picnickers.

Debbie eyed the feasts of the numerous diners. "Ooh, I'm starved."

"And a good thing too." Greg beamed. "I'd hate to think my carefully laid plans had gone for nothing."

"What?"

"While you, my Sleeping Beauty, were undoubtedly still cozy between your covers, we were out and about. Weren't we, Melissa?" Melissa giggled and nodded. "One thing about this kid, she knows how to keep a secret. We tucked a lunch basket from the deli in the trunk of my car before we brought it over this morning."

Debbie felt enormous relief. She had wondered about getting home. She couldn't imagine walking all that way over the hill again. "But how did you get back?"

"Remember Charlie the plumber? He services several places on the mountain—cabins back in the woods with aging plumbing. He met us and took us back. These outings require the logistics of a major military campaign."

"Well, I can't tell you how glad I am we don't have to walk back." Debbie flopped down on the lush green grass. She closed her eyes for what couldn't have been more than a few seconds. And opened them to find a banquet spread before her. "Wow! Magic!" She rolled to a sitting position.

The sandwiches were Lebanese mountain bread stuffed to the bursting point with ham, turkey, beef, cheeses, lettuce, pickles, and tomatoes. And they were accompanied with deviled eggs, pickled beets, sweet purple plums, huge chocolate cookies, and a Thermos of lemonade. "This is incredible. You do know how to order a picnic."

"They had a great-looking chocolate fudge cake. It broke my heart that they couldn't cram it in the basket too."

"Well, next time have them put the cake in first. After all, what's important?" She spoke lightly, but part of her mind couldn't help wondering if there would be a next time. She couldn't keep up the battle forever. Sooner or later . . .

But as she leaned back on the sun-warmed blanket something else was tickling her mind. A question she couldn't quite form into words. Yet something was keeping her mind from being as contented as her stomach. She looked at Greg as she puzzled. It didn't seem that the annoying insect of a thought had anything to do with him. And yet . . . Something of importance had happened. It was the feeling of having forgotten someone's birthday but not being able to remember whose . . . of knowing you'd promised a friend you'd do something but couldn't remember what it was.

But then, if it didn't have anything to do with Greg, it couldn't be very important, could it?

Melissa's energy level was, of course, restored first. The last crumbs of the picnic barely disappeared before she wanted to go exploring. Greg just groaned and stretched his long form out on the blanket newly cleared of the repast.

"I think I spotted some blackberry bushes just beyond the trail over there." Debbie nodded her head toward a mound of tangled green bushes. "Bring the basket. We'll go gather blackberries while your daddy has a rest."

Greg gave a lazy grin in approval of the plan as Melissa skipped toward the trail. Debbie hurried after her. "I'll be Flopsy. Do you want to be Mopsy or Cottontail?"

"Who're they?"

"My goodness, don't you know Peter Rabbit?" When Melissa shook her head Debbie realized this child's bedtime stories were sadly in need of an enrichment program. The branches laden with fat, rich blackberries glistened like ebony in the sun. As they piled the fruit into the basket Debbie began: "Once upon a time there were four little rabbits, and their names were Flopsy, Mopsy, Cottontail, and Peter. They lived with their mother in a sandbank underneath the root of a very big fir tree . . ."

She glanced down at Melissa and saw that her fingers were rapidly getting as black as the inside of the basket. "Don't squeeze them, honey. Just pull gently and pop them into the basket—or your mouth." Even as full as Debbie was after lunch, the succulent berries were irresistible. She slipped a couple in her mouth before continuing, ". . . so one day their mother said, 'Run along, now. But don't get into mischief. I am going out.' Flopsy, Mopsy, and Cottontail were good little bunnies. So they went down the lane to gather blackberries . . ."

"Just like us!"

"That's right." The sun was warm on Debbie's back and head, the surf rolled on the beach below the cliff, and she was filled with a sense of rightness and peace that she wanted to clasp to herself forever. The privilege of introducing a child to Beatrix Potter was something very precious. Others could wrestle with the issues of war and peace, world hunger, and human rights—someone had to—but her ministry was closer to home, and, in a microscopic way, the issues were the same. ". . . His mother put Peter to bed. She made some chamomile tea and gave a dose of it to Peter. But Flopsy, Mopsy, and Cottontail had bread and milk and blackberries for supper."

"Yes, we are good bunnies!" Melissa said with a mouth stained a dark purple/black to show she had followed Debbie's example of sampling the wares.

"And I'm the Big Bad Wolf." A gravely voice came from behind them.

Debbie laughed. "I see your daughter isn't the only one whose education has been neglected. There's no Big Bad Wolf in *The Tale of Peter Rabbit*—just a big bad Mr. McGregor." Hands on her hips, she surveyed Greg through narrowed eyes. "And somehow, you don't seem typecast for the role."

"If you saw my woeful attempts at gardening, you'd be certain of it."

Debbie held the brimming basket out to him. He took a handful, eating them like popcorn as she said, "I commiserate. I had such great ambitions, but all my vegetables died. Even zucchini, and everybody in the world can grow zucchini. I didn't feel quite so bad about my corn, at least I had the excuse that our soil was straight sand, and corn needs rich loam."

A little, nostalgic smile played around the corners of her mouth as she continued, "Now flowers are a different matter. I had great daylilies and daisies and mums. And I kept on with the beds of pansies, columbine, and snapdragons Mother and I planted together. Partly because I loved them and partly because I felt they should be Angie and Andy's heritage too. I can't imagine growing up without having snapdragons to clip on the ends of your fingers in the summer."

"You could always substitute black olives." Greg wiggled his fingers as if sporting impromptu puppets.

"That was one thing Mother never allowed. But I let the twins. Olives just don't taste as good any other way. Besides, there's a kind of logic to it. You have five olives on your fingers, then you eat one, and that leaves four—maybe I'd have a better sense of math today if my mother had worried less about table manners."

"I don't think your mother left much room for improvement." Greg had become suddenly serious.

"My mother! What do you know about her? About the mess she left?" Debbie turned and stalked back toward the picnic spot.

Greg caught up with her at the top of the path. "Debbie, I'm sorry if I said the wrong thing. I don't know anything. But I wish I did. I wish you'd open up to me."

"No you don't. Ignorance is bliss. Besides, there *isn't* anything." She shook the blanket with heated energy, then folded it with meticulous precision.

Greg waited until her composure returned. "Er, how about a run into Cannon Beach? You haven't been downtown, have you?"

Like Seaside, the little town of Cannon Beach was only one street wide. They walked the length of the town on the wooden verandas of old-west style buildings feeling as if they were on a movie set. But no western movie was ever decorated so riotously. Wooden tubs spilled their contents of bright pink and white petunias at the strollers' feet while hanging baskets overflowed above their heads. Melissa looked longingly at the pink and white awninged candy shop, but Greg shook his head. "Not now, Punkin. There's something better up ahead."

Gift shops and art galleries beckoned to them with promises of pleasant browsing, but it was the heady scents from the bakery next to the old-fashioned ice cream parlor that lured them in. "They make the world's best chocolate eclairs here." Greg pointed to the cases overflowing with goodies.

"Is that based on personal research?" Debbie asked.

"Sounds like a worthwhile project." Greg took a number for order of service. "But when you find the ultimate you know it."

Debbie caught her breath at the note of double entendre in his quiet voice. Even as she smiled, a trickle of fear ran down her spine. If he knew . . . Had she made a terrible mistake in determining to enjoy the day? "No matter how ultimate they are, I couldn't possibly eat a thing right now."

"I know. We'll take them home for supper."

"Do you always plan such well-balanced meals?"

"Only when I'm dieting."

"Well, at least we have the blackberries. Oh, and I've got some sourdough bread and low fat cheese," Debbie said.

"And are you always so well prepared?"

"My senior year in college I received home management credit for my work at home. I had to be prepared for the department head to drop in any time and see what I was serving for dinner. I was a nervous wreck all term just knowing she'd pick the one night I'd burned the stew and was out of lettuce."

"Did she?"

"She only popped in once. It was roast chicken with fresh green beans, so my honor was safe."

The aproned girl behind the counter called Greg's number. Soon they were on their way back to Seaside, Melissa sitting guard by the white pastry box in the backseat.

"I think we can manage to keep out of the eclairs for a couple of hours, but after that you take your chances." Greg told Debbie as she jumped out of the car at her cottage.

When she opened the kitchen door a fat mosquito entered with her and began buzzing irritatingly around the room.

"Just you wait. I'll get you." Debbie rolled up an old newspaper and began swatting. But the saucy insect escaped her best shots. She tossed the paper on the table. It fell open to reveal the headline she remembered all too well announcing Councilman Larsen's death.

With the thick black letters bringing back visions of that catastrophe and the buzzing sound still flying around her head, the idea that had eluded Debbie all afternoon slipped into focus. The boy at Indian Beach accused his friend of overriding the controls on the plane. Was it possible that the freak accident that killed Duane Larsen *wasn't* an accident?

Chapter 11

Debbie blinked, trying to assimilate the implications of such a thought. But surely the authorities would have taken charge if there had been the least hint of foul play. And there were all those witnesses—there must have been at least 25 people watching. Yet the paper had carried not a single suggestion of anything irregular.

Well, Ryland had been there. She would ask him what he thought when he got back from Salem—if he called her as he said he would. The mosquito landed on her neck. Debbie slapped it, squashing blood all over her fingers. The sight made her shiver as it blended with remembered red stains on the sand.

When she picked up the newspaper she saw what it had covered. Byrl, as usual, had left a note saying not to wait up for her. *She should write one note and put it out every evening,* Debbie thought. After all, they all said the same thing. But of more interest was a letter from Angie. Debbie wanted to give her full attention, so she set it aside for a minute while she drew a nice hot bath. She would probably have to read between the lines to determine how Angie really felt about her pregnancy. Debbie wanted to be sure her sister was sure. All she had ever wanted was the best for Angie. Debbie would do anything—she had done everything—for her sister's happiness. Nothing must spoil it now.

Debbie sank back in the hot, bubbly water and opened Angie's letter. After reading only a few lines and glancing at the border filled with hasty sketches of hearts, flowers, and smiles, she knew the letter had been written in a state of euphoria. Angie's joy simply leapt off the page as she told in great detail about her new maternity clothes, their plans for the baby, what Ron said, what the doctor said, how she planned to decorate the nursery . . .

". . . Tell Byrl hi for me. How do you like living with a celebrity?

> Love from your fat sister,
> Angie"

Debbie let the letter drop by the side of the tub. Well, OK—that certainly did seem to be right for Angie. But she was so young. Angie wasn't much older than . . .

But, good grief, Angela did go on a bit. Didn't say a thing about Dad and Leonora, or the house or the weather.

Angie's letter also made her long to hear from Andy. Her tall, lanky brother with the mop of brown hair that always fell in his eyes never wrote letters, but they usually called each other occasionally. The last time she had talked to him was at their father's wedding in June. And Debbie had sensed a little dissatisfaction in him then. In the bustle of family comings and goings there had been no time to really talk. Maybe if she dressed quickly she could take time just to call and say hello.

She pulled a soft rose sweater on over her turtleneck and jeans. With a few practiced flicks of her brush and the help of several sturdy pins she twisted her long black hair to the top of her head, then shivered as the tendrils curling along her neck tickled her. A hint of blusher and honey rose lipstick and she was still under the two-hour limit decreed by Greg.

The phone rang several times at the other end of the line. Debbie had almost decided Andy was out when his boyish voice came down the wire. "Andy! It's so good to hear your voice! How are you?"

"Sis? Hey, is that really you?" he sounded glad to hear her too. "I'm, uh, fine. Just fine."

"Andy, I heard that hesitation. What gives?"

"I really am fine, just surprised by your call because I'd been thinking about you."

"It won't do, Andy. Don't hold out on me when I'm paying the long-distance charges."

"OK, Sis, but don't hit the ceiling." She heard him take a breath. "I'm thinking of not going back to college this fall."

"What!"

"I told you not to hit the ceiling. Look, I've got a good job here—not great, but a job—which is more than a lot of college graduates have these days. It seems dumb to quit to go back to school when I really don't know what I want to take. I mean, I'm almost 20 years old, and I don't know what I really want to do in life. It'll be an awful waste if I study the wrong stuff."

"But, Andy, that job's a dead end. You could be there 20 years and still just be working in the stockroom. What better way is there to find out what you want to do than to study different fields?"

"Yeah, you may be right. I'll think about it. Say, isn't that something about ol' Angie?"

"Yes. It certainly is. I have to go, Andy. Bye."

Greg seemed to sense her depression almost as soon as she arrived. But he didn't question her until they were comfortably sitting around big bowls of blackberries with a tray of sharp cheese and crusty French bread. "Want to talk about it? Whatever's troubling you—"

Not until she heard his words did she realize how very much she did want to talk. She had thought earlier of calling her father, but it seemed unfair to burden him when he was so happy. "Yes. I do. I didn't realize it was so obvious." He smiled and waited for her to go on at her own pace. "It's Andy. I called him just before coming over. He's thinking of not going back to school. He says he thinks he should just keep on with the job he's got. Stocking shelves in a discount store. Can you imagine? And he's *brilliant!* I got him through every accelerated class that high school offered. Reviewed him for quizzes, proofread his papers, read assignments to him when he was too tired to read himself. All that so he could be a stock clerk?

"I had a perfect schedule worked out for him—for all four years of college. A business and economics major. So he could either get his masters or go into business with Dad when he graduated. And last year he did just fine. What's the matter with him? How could he so suddenly go off the rails like that?"

"Sounds like you had his life all worked out for him."

"Of course I did. It was my job to take care of him. I did everything I possibly could."

"And I'm sure you did it brilliantly."

"Well, I did my best. Hot breakfasts. Clean jeans, ironed shirts. Regular study hours."

Greg nodded. "But did you ever ask him what he wanted to do?"

"Of course I did. But he would never say. He wasn't like Angie. She always stood up to me—told me what she was going to do and that was that. No matter how clearly I showed her she was wrong. And see what's come of it—having a baby at her age. I had to make Andy's decisions for him. It was my job."

"And now he wants to take it on for himself."

"And make a mess of it. I'm gone for less than two months and look what happens."

Greg was quiet for a moment. "Did Andy ever talk about what he wanted to do? When he was younger?"

"You mean after the Power Ranger and G.I. Joe stages? Well, when he was in the third or fourth grade he used to talk about being a missionary to South America. Which was pretty surprising, because he hardly knew where South America was at that age."

"Did he do anything about that?"

Debbie shrugged. "Read adventure books set south of the border. Took a lot of Spanish. But he never talked about it anymore. That's why I told him to major in business."

"You told him?"

"Advised him, yes. It was my job to guide him. And after all—missionaries make no money, and it can be awfully dangerous . . ."

"You always fought his battles for him."

"Of course."

"I think this is one he'll have to battle out for himself. We can help, though."

"We?"

When he held his hands out across the table Melissa instantly dropped her spoon and put her hand in her daddy's. "We already prayed, Daddy. Did you forget something?"

Debbie supposed it all helped—talking to Greg, praying for Andy—but she couldn't get rid of the compulsion inside her that she should *do* something. Get on the first plane to Boise and sort it all out. What if Andrew and Angela really messed up? What if they didn't do things right? They had to be the best. It all had to be perfect for them.

· "And now for the pièce de résistance." Greg placed an eclair before each of them. They were large, the *pâte à chou* shell filled with rich, French pastry cream and the top generously spread with a smooth, milk chocolate icing.

Debbie could think of nothing better to drown her worries with. She took a big bite and savored the delicate flavors while Greg and Melissa waited for her reaction. She made a face. "Terrible!" she reached across the table and grabbed their plates. "I'll just take these home to dispose of them so you won't feel obligated to eat them." Melissa gave a shriek of laugher, and Greg picked up his fork to defend his property.

In a few minutes a thin rim of chocolate around Melissa's mouth was all that was left as evidence—not even a telltale crumb on anyone's plate. "OK, I'll say it." Debbie grinned. "That was the ultimate."

"Thought you'd never admit it." Then his mind made one of those rapid shifts she had seen him do so often. "I keep forgetting to ask you. Did you ever find your compact?"

"Oh!" Debbie's hands flew to her face. "How could I

have forgotten? I meant to call the very next morning. Then I never gave it another thought. Oh, I do hope I'm not too late. Surely the janitor would have found it by now."

Melissa's head was drooping almost to the table. "Time to get ready for bed, Punkin. It's been a full day for you, and you have Sunday School in the morning."

"You go brush your teeth and put your pajamas on," Debbie said. "Then I'll come tell you a story. Would you like to hear Peter Rabbit again?"

Melissa nodded and slid to her feet. Greg began gathering the dishes. "Here, let me." Debbie jumped up.

A strong, warm hand clasped her shoulder. "Sit, woman. You think I can't handle this?"

Debbie didn't even get her mouth open to reply when the glass he had stacked precariously in a bowl toppled to the floor with a crash and splintered. They were still laughing when Melissa, clutching a teddy bear, padded back in. "No bare feet in here." Debbie scooped her up in her arms. "Your daddy's demonstrating the caveman method of dishwashing, but he doesn't seem to have it quite perfected yet."

"That's all right, you can laugh now. But I'll get the bugs worked out. It'll revolutionize the industry."

"That's right," Debbie replied from the next room. "The dish manufacturing industry."

When she returned from Melissa's bedroom, Greg was waiting for her, sitting on one end of the sofa with his long legs stretched out in front of him. She started to take the chair across from him but he stopped her. "Sit over here."

She moved to the end of the sofa. "Here, I said." He patted the cushion next to him. "What is this standoff bit?"

"I wasn't intending to stand. You stopped my sitting twice."

"Debbie, no nonsense now. I've been trying to talk to you all day, but we kept getting interrupted." He put his arm around her.

Nonsense was the farthest thing from her mind as she

turned to him, waiting to hear what he wanted to talk about.

"I want to know how you feel. About me."

She opened her mouth to answer, but no words came out. Her throat closed and her stomach knotted. All she could do was shake her head as she pulled away. He let her go.

"I thought so. It's Shawn, isn't it?"

"No. No, not Shawn. Not him."

"No. Not as a person. I mean it's what Shawn did to you."

Her eyes on the floor, her nod was almost imperceptible. "Deborah, if I were a professional counselor it would be highly improper for me to advise you. Fortunately, that's no longer part of my job, because I very much want to tell you something. And you can think of this as coming from a detached, professional doctor or from the man who loves you. But either way it's true."

The man who loves you. The man who— Debbie clapped both hands over her mouth and pushed herself into the corner of the sofa, curling her legs under her. The conflicting urges to throw herself into his arms and to fight and scream tore at her.

"That's all right. Don't say anything. Just listen." His voice was so calming. She focused on that. His voice. Just listen to his voice.

"Debbie, we need to talk about this false shame you're carrying. It really isn't your fault that you were raped. You have to understand that so you can forgive yourself. Rape always leaves the victim feeling soiled and worthless. But rape—"

"I wasn't—" Her muttered words barely cut across his.

"What?"

"I said, I wasn't raped." She took a breath, then almost shouted it. *"I wasn't raped!"*

Greg sat in silence as the words fell to the floor and splintered.

"I told myself I was. I had to. I tried to believe it. I

couldn't admit even to myself that I had wanted—even asked for Shawn to love me."

Greg still didn't say anything. She had to go on. Fill the silence with words. "My mother was *dying*. My world had fallen apart. We were so close. I had forgotten how close my mother and I were until this time with Melissa. I guess I shut it out because the memories were too painful."

She took a deep breath to steady herself. Now that she'd started, the words were pushing at each other to get out. All that shameful truth she had kept bottled up inside her for so long. Now it all spilled over. She couldn't have stopped if she'd tried. "I was desperate for something to hold to. And there was Shawn. He was a good, gentle person. He really cared about me. And he was there; and my mother was leaving me." She shook her head. "He was so sweet.

"And then I realized what I'd done. It wasn't at all what I wanted. I started screaming and hitting." She flailed at the sofa cushions with both hands. Hitting and sobbing. The pins came out of her hair. It fell across her shoulders as she jerked her head back and forth. "No, no. Don't touch me! Rape. Rape. Rape!" The sobs tore from her throat as she buried her face in her hands.

"But we both knew it wasn't rape." Suddenly she looked up. "I did a terrible thing to Shawn, too, didn't I? A terrible thing. But what can I do? I did a terrible thing, but I can't undo it." She lay back against the sofa, drained. Dark straggles of hair clung to her wet forehead.

"No, you can't undo it. But there are things you can do."

She looked at him, waiting. She would do anything. Inside she felt like she was in the middle of spring cleaning—dumping all the junk out of her bureau drawers. The top drawer was clean and empty. But there was still that pile of junk on the bed to be sorted and arranged.

"You need forgiveness. Have you asked God to forgive you?"

"Over and over. You don't know how many times."

"Then He has. You believe that, don't you?"

She nodded. She believed it with her head. She didn't believe it with her heart, because her heart knew she wasn't worthy of being forgiven. Fortunately, Greg didn't probe.

"Then you need the forgiveness of the other person you hurt."

"Shawn?"

"That's right. Have you ever told him you're sorry?"

"I never saw him again. We went to different high schools, different churches. He called when my mother died. I never returned his message."

"Do you know where he is now?"

"No. I think his parents still live in Boise. He might be married, but I haven't heard." She hunched her shoulders.

"If you could write him a letter, it would do you both a lot of good."

"Both?"

"Yes. Owning responsibility for what happened is a crucial recovery step. You've started by admitting it to me. Now you need to admit it to him. And freeing him from that responsibility will help him with any guilt he may be carrying."

"If he is married, it could help his marriage?"

"Definitely."

Greg walked her home without talking, without touching her. She sat long at the kitchen table with her pen in her hand. In the end, there really wasn't so much to say. She explained as clearly as she could what had happened, both on that night so long ago, and now to bring her to accepting this responsibility. She hoped he could forgive her, and she wished him well. She read it through three times, decided it would have to do, and wrote Shawn Miller on the envelope. She put it inside a larger envelope addressed to her father with a note asking that he forward the letter.

She held it out and looked at it. What had she really said? How did she feel about it? She had done what she had to do. She didn't really feel much of anything. She set it aside.

There. That was done. An entire turning point of her life dealt with. That drawer wasn't in perfect order yet, but she had the contents sorted. She sat on the edge of her bed, staring at the Trezadone tablet. After such a long, emotional day she needed it. She doubted there had been a day in the past six years when she had needed it more. And she really couldn't take having her sleep filled with bleeding, broken, crying dolls. Surely, if she could ever be justified in taking refuge in drugs, it would be tonight.

And yet something held her back. It wasn't the pill. Doctor Hilde had assured her it was perfectly safe. A very common prescription for sleep disturbances. And yet, after such painfully honest peeling away of her defenses, it seemed like a step backward to use a chemical to blot out her dreams. In the end she took one out of the bottle and left it on her nightstand with a glass of water beside it. Just in case.

She slept until daylight. And wakened with a sense of aloneness and loss. And yet a great awareness of love. She lay for a long time, trying to bring the images back. Like the melody of a half-forgotten song one strains to remember and finds just beyond their grasp, the vision eluded her.

Then she remembered. In a rush it flooded over her. And Debbie did something she hadn't done since she was a teenager. She grabbed the pen and notepad by her bedside and wrote a poem, just as it came to her, complete as the realization of the dream.

> *My mother came to me last night.*
> *She stood at the door and held a towel.*
> *"Come in from the rain,*
> *You'll catch cold."*
> *She held me in her arms,*
> *My head on her narrow chest.*
> *She was always so thin.*
> *I could even hear her breathe.*

I felt her love.
Felt it flow through me,
Tangible and warm.
I relaxed in her arms
Like a small girl back home again.
I awoke.
She was gone.
She had been so close,
So very dear.
Why did she come back from heaven afar
To hold her daughter in her arms?

Debbie read it again. Where had the words come from? She looked at the pen in her hand. Was that hers?

She was loved and comforted. By her mother. She folded the paper and tucked it in the back of her Bible.

And Greg had said he loved her. Words she had never thought she would hear. But now that she had heard them, she had to face the responsibility. Last night she had accepted the responsibility of Shawn's having loved her. But what of her mother's love? Could she take that responsibility? What of Greg's?

She only knew that she didn't feel up to facing Greg right then, so she went to a little church in Seaside rather than driving over to Cannon Beach as she knew he and Melissa would be doing. Then, by spending the rest of the day indoors like a mole, she managed to avoid him. Byrl was hibernating too. Not just in the house, but in her room, so that, what with worrying about Andy between times of trying to sort out her own perplexities, this was not one of Debbie's better days.

And the next day was no better—definitely a leading candidate for the Blue Monday award. Debbie stowed the results of her shopping expedition for Greg's birthday dinner in her refrigerator as she thought over the situation. What she needed was more perspective—a little distance.

She looked at the stalk of celery in her hand. *Yeah, and cooking for him is a great way to achieve distance.* Well, Ryland was due back from Salem soon. Maybe he would provide a change of scenery.

Debbie pushed the refrigerator door shut and listened. It seemed that Byrl's computer was going slower and slower. Finally it quit altogether. After a silence that seemed more oppressive than just a pause to look up a research note, Byrl emerged from her room and headed straight for the coffeepot.

"You look awful." Debbie surveyed her cousin's sallow complexion and the dark lines under her eyes.

"Thanks. I'd return the compliment, but at the moment my eyes are too bleary to know."

It was obvious that all was not well in Ms. Byrl Coffman's world. But Debbie didn't know what to say, so she just finished stowing the last of her purchases and sat at the table with a cup of coffee she didn't really want, waiting for her cousin to talk.

"So, tell me. How's Adonis and Little Miss Muffet?"

Debbie avoided a direct answer. "Tomorrow's his birthday. I'm fixing dinner. It's supposed to be a surprise."

"The proverbial way to a man's heart." It was very nearly a sneer.

Debbie shrugged. Her emotions were much too confused at the moment to attempt defending anything she did.

"Well, one thing I can say for your Victorian ideas of not giving him anything more than food before they sing 'O Promise Me' is that at least you don't feel like quite such a *fool* when you get dumped flat on your, er—back. Pardon the reference."

"Do you want to talk about it?"

"I just did. What else is there to say? There were no promises asked, given, or taken. But the louse could have warned me before I decided to pop in on him Saturday that I was in danger of finding *another woman* there with him."

Byrl drank deeply of her coffee. "There *are moments* when one wonders what's the point of it all . . ." She shrugged and tossed her head. "So, this is one of those moments. It'll pass and leave ye olde sadder-but-wiser me in its wake."

Byrl grew up spending as much time in Sunday School as Debbie had, and she could probably have quoted more Bible verses than Debbie. So she didn't need any sermons. Not ones of words. Just actions. "You need a change of scenery." Debbie jumped to her feet. "What'll it be—swimming? shopping? beachcombing?"

Byrl looked at her in surprise. "You serious? You don't have plans?"

Debbie shook her head. "Nothing as important as you." She gave her cousin an impetuous hug. To her surprise it was returned.

"Well, what I really need to do is to run up to Astoria and visit Fort Clatsop where Sacajawea spent the winter with the Lewis and Clark party."

"Great. Let's go. I'll drive so you can be free to take notes along the way."

It was a quick drive northward to the oldest city in the Pacific Northwest at the mouth of the Columbia River. At the reconstructed fort, the original of which the explorers completed on Christmas Eve, 1805, the cousins walked slowly around the heavy stockade walls and spent some time in the captain's living quarters, trying to imagine what the winter must have been like for the young Indian woman living there with her infant son.

They took a trail leading from the fort to the canoe landing on the Lewis and Clark River. "What did Sacajawea do after the expedition?" Debbie asked.

"She went back to St. Louis with Charboneau, her husband. I haven't found out yet what happened to him, but she lived for a long time on the Wind River Reservation in Wyoming. I read that she died in 1884, but I haven't learned yet just what she did. One disadvantage of working in a small town is the limited library resources. But I'll dig it all out. Sacajawea is becoming a favorite of mine. I may even do a book on her later. Do you *realize* she was only *18* when she made the trip with Lewis and Clark?"

Debbie looked up from the replica of the dugout canoe she was studying. "No. I didn't know. And with a baby. He must have been an incredible inconvenience, yet she did it." She was quiet while Byrl made a lengthy note. "Do any of your sources mention whether or not Sacajawea had any Christian training?"

Byrl looked at her for a moment. "Good question. I would never have thought of that." She scratched another note. "Sometimes I wonder if there's something to this 'Faith of Our Fathers' thing."

Debbie nodded. So did she.

Chapter 12

The next morning Debbie was just taking a puffy white meringue crust from the oven when she heard a knock at the door.

Greg and Melissa stood there. "We've decided to celebrate my birthday by going blading."

"Um, blading?"

"Rollerblading. In-line skates." Greg started to explain.

"Yeah, sure. I know what they are. I'm a mole, but I live on this planet. I guess I hadn't figured that would be your thing. Whatever next? skateboarding? skydiving?"

Greg grinned and held up a hand. "Whoa. One thing at a time, please. I have to do something to prove I'm not completely over the hill at 35. But I do want to survive the day. Want to come watch me break my neck?"

"What you mean is you want me there to fall on." Debbie could hear her heart pounding. She hadn't seen him since Saturday night—two and a half days. Now she knew how it must feel to go to a cocktail party when you were trying to stay on the wagon. All that distance she was trying to gain suddenly lost its attraction. "Er, I don't have any skates—blades, that is."

Greg produced a pair from behind his back. "Surprise."

She pulled back. If they were Gayle's, she didn't want to have anything to do with trying to fill her shoes—or rollerblades.

"We rented them when we got ours," Greg said.

Debbie eyed the size 7 stamped on the heel. "How did you know my size?"

"You left a pair of slippers in the spa room. We took them with us."

"I found them." Melissa looked terribly proud of herself as she held out the missing slippers.

Debbie laughed. "So that's where those went to. I'd wondered. OK, give me a minute." She ducked into her room and slipped a high-necked, dusty blue sweater on over her light blue jeans and tied her hair back with a blue and white scarf.

She sat on the front steps to lace up her skates while Greg, holding tight to Melissa, instructed her on handling the wheels under her feet. Debbie couldn't help noticing how, even on an overcast morning, Greg managed to look as if the sun were shining on him. "Show-off," she said, noting the way he was dressed.

"What do you mean?" he offered his hand to help her stand up.

"Roller-skating in shorts is like doing crossword puzzles in ink."

He shook his head. "Your mistake. I figured my knees could grow new skin easier than my jeans could grow patches."

Debbie had roller-skated and ice-skated as a child, so she adapted quickly to the rollerblading sensation. As soon as she caught her balance she enjoyed the greater freedom of having the wheels in a line rather than in a rectangle under her feet. For a while they bladed with Melissa between them, but soon she caught the sense of it and struck out on her own. The wheels on the rough cement tickled the bottoms of Debbie's feet, making her giggle. "I haven't done anything like this since I was in junior high. It's great!"

Children zoomed by them on bicycles and skateboards, elderly couples strolled along hand-in-hand, young parents pushed babies in strollers or carried them in backpacks, and every third person they met had a dog on a leash. Debbie waved an arm at it all. "What would Seaside be without the Prom?"

"It's practically a symbol of the city," Greg agreed. "I read in *The Signal* last week that the city fathers are considering some repairs to it. The most minor repairs will cost several times the $150,000 the whole thing cost in 1923."

"I wish I could have seen it then." Debbie gave him a mischievous grin. "Tell me what it was like. You must remember it."

"Now you've gone too far. I beat students for less that that." He reached for her.

She pushed just beyond his grasp, her wheels clacking over each seam in the cement. "You'll have to catch me first," she called over her shoulder.

She managed to keep ahead of him for a while, weaving skillfully around strollers who smiled at her. But she couldn't keep up the effort for long. Finally she surrendered, clinging to the balustrade, laughing and gasping for breath. "I give up." She held up her hand in defense. "Please don't beat me, kind sir."

He twirled an imaginary mustache and raised his eyebrows. "And what makes you think I'm kind?"

"I was trying to appeal to your better nature—it must be in there somewhere. But as a last resort I can scream a lot."

He threw up his hands. "Now *that* appeals to my better nature. Can you imagine the item in *The Signal?* 'Dr. Gregory Masefield of Pacific Evangelical Seminary was arrested today for accosting a beautiful young woman on the Promenade. "I couldn't help myself," Masefield said in defense. When the judge saw the woman, Miss Deborah Ann Jensen of Boise, Idaho, he declared himself in sympathy with Masefield and released him to the custody of Miss Jensen.'"

"You are a nut." Debbie giggled. "What do I want with custody of you?"

"That's what I keep wondering." The teasing was gone from Greg's blue eyes. "But you're going to have to decide, you know."

Unable to meet his gaze, Debbie pushed ahead to catch up with Melissa. At the kiosk they bought caramel corn and saltwater taffy and sat on a brick bench overlooking the beach as they munched. Across the broad expanse of beach, holidayers engaged in various activities. Several groups of children dug in the sand, one near them laughing as they buried the largest boy up to his neck. Early sun-worshipers, still clad in sweatshirts, staked out their territory in anticipation of sunnier times. Kite fliers awaited the breeze that would clear the sky for the sun, one with a giant dragon kite spread out on the sand like a fallen rainbow. Farther out, on the damp, surf-washed beach, groups of sand cycle riders sped up and down, looking like a horde of sand crabs, and on the dunes off to their left someone flew a gasoline powered plane. Debbie shivered. "I'll always hate those things."

"I understand your feelings. But try not to let it bother you. Freak accidents happen."

"I know. But that's what worries me . . ."

"What?"

She spoke quietly. She didn't want Melissa to overhear. "The thing is, I'm not absolutely convinced it *was* an accident."

Greg frowned. "What else could it have been?"

"Well, remember those guys arguing at Indian Beach about how one of them overrode the commands of the pilot with another set of controls?" Greg nodded. Debbie took another deep breath. "Well the next morning I was walking on the beach and found a radio control. I assumed it was the one Larsen was using, except for one funny thing. It was on the other side of the dune from where he was."

"Maybe a kid carried if off."

"Exactly what I thought. But I don't know—he was such an important man—the kind that could be a target for something, I suppose."

"What did you do with the control?"

"I met Ryland Carlsburg a little later and showed it to him. He offered to get it back to Larsen's family."

"Well, there you are then. If there was anything wrong, the family would have noticed and told the police."

"Yeah, I suppose so . . ."

"Daddy, I'm thirsty." Melissa threw her caramel corn bag in the litter barrel.

Their sweet snack had left them all thirsty, so they lined up at the drinking fountain before blading on. Soon past the motels on the south end of the Prom, Debbie admired the flower-bordered lawns facing the ocean. The cool, moist climate produced such intense color in the flowers that a small bed or single pot could light up a whole yard. Debbie called Greg's attention to a luminous hedge of red geraniums four feet high. Then she paused before a display of fluorescent-colored tuberous begonias, some of the blooms as big as paper plates. "I can't believe that." She shook her head. "My whole plants don't get as big as one of those blossoms. It's a good thing my mother told me to expect life to be unfair—it prepares one for such disappointments."

"You really have a green thumb, don't you?"

"Well, it's more a green heart. Green thumb implies success. I just have good intentions. I always dreamed of doing a really old-fashioned garden with hollyhocks and daisies and morning glories. I suppose in my apartment I'll have to be content with misting a fern and growing a pot of chives in the kitchen." She was quiet for a moment. "But I do love growing things."

The further they left the town behind them on their two mile course, the heavier the wild vegetation grew on the beach side as well. Hillocks of rolling sand dunes were covered with thick beach grass, scrubby gnarled bushes, and tall, slim-stemmed dandelions that nodded in the breeze like daisies.

The wind everyone waited for appeared on cue to sweep the clouds from the sky. Now a warm sun shone on the skaters. Much too warm. Debbie regretted her heavy sweater as sticky prickles irritated her neck and arms. No matter how stoically she tried to ignore it, the discomfort increased. She looked with envy at Greg and Melissa whose recently shed windbreakers were tied loosely over their cotton shirts. She longed for a breath of cool breeze to find its way inside her wool sweater. It became an endurance test, and she was losing.

Debbie argued with herself for a block further, then gave up. "Greg, I feel so stupid, but this sweater is killing me. Could I, er, could I borrow your windbreaker?" The beach bracken now provided solid cover, and little trails led off through the brush, beckoning her to a private dressing room.

Greg sketched a bow. "My jacket would be honored."

The rollerblades necessitated making her way carefully on the tiny, sandy trail, but it wasn't many steps until she could sink behind a screening hedge. The relief as she wriggled out of the sticky sweater was almost equal to the temptation to sit there half dressed in the fresh air. Only the fear of someone coming along the path made her hurry. Then she froze. Someone was coming.

She heard voices approaching from the beach side. Should she scramble into the jacket or stay still and not attract any attention? The voices stopped a few feet from her just beyond the bushes. Hushed, intense tones made her hold her breath.

"A whole percent apiece? For each of the six—er, five of us?"

"That's what he said."

"Just for the promise not to push for a public vote?"

"That's right. Just sign the thing in the routine course of business."

"Let me think about it."

"Fine. Just don't take too long."

Footsteps muffled by the sand faded away. Debbie scrambled into her newly acquired attire. The cool, slick feel of the white nylon windbreaker restored her comfort and her energy, and she felt only minimally foolish when she emerged in the jacket that hung halfway to her knees.

"Cute." Greg held out his hand to help her back onto the Prom. "Let that be a lesson to you. Always dress in layers at the beach."

Somehow the clownish outfit produced a playful mood. Debbie laughed and raced off toward the end of the Prom. She loved the sense of freedom as she pushed hard for several strides, then coasted—sometimes crouching like a skier, sometimes with her arms out as if flying. This was great. A wonderful sense of freedom engulfed her.

She really was free. She had finished her obligations at home. Free. She had made her peace with Shawn. Free. There was nothing holding her back. But . . . Nothing. Nothing do you hear? She was free.

On the way back home they detoured down a side street marked Lewis and Clark Way to visit the salt cairn where, Greg explained to Melissa after refreshing his memory by reading the markers, three men from the exploration party had worked for two months during the winter of 1806, keeping the fires burning constantly in order to boil 1,400 gallons of seawater to make salt for the journey.

"Why did they need salt?" Melissa asked.

"To cure their meat," Debbie answered. "They didn't have freezers or canning then."

Melissa regarded her with a frown. "Was the meat sick?"

Debbie bit her lip to keep from laughing at the child's question. "No, but the people would have been if they hadn't fixed their meat with salt to keep it from spoiling."

"Then why did you say . . ."

Greg came to Debbie's rescue. "Come over here, Punkin. You can see better on this side."

They bladed around the black wrought iron fence and gazed through the rails at the oblong stone oven supporting five big black "kittles" of water. Debbie shook her head. "What a lot of work. Just to produce four bushels of salt."

"The saltmakers were really the first white residents of

Seaside." Then Greg turned to Melissa. "A little Clatsop Indian girl named Jenny Michael helped the people find the right place to rebuild this display because her father told her how he remembered seeing the white men working here."

But Melissa's attention span for historical detail was expended, so they skated homeward, moving more slowly and with more frequent rest stops than on the outward trip. They finally rolled in, pulling Melissa between them. "If you'll take a nap now, honey, maybe your daddy will let you come over for another cooking lesson when you get up." Debbie gave her young accomplice a surreptitious wink, then handed her rollerblades back to Greg.

"OK. Then daddy can come get me. I'm taking him to Norma's for his birthday dinner." Melissa replied right on cue. That went even better than they had rehearsed it.

Greg held out his hand to Melissa, suppressing a yawn. "Mmm, all this exercise and fresh air was supposed to stimulate my brain for a round of writing. But somehow the idea of a nap is almost overwhelming."

"Why not, Gramps? Seniors always nap in the afternoon, don't they?" Debbie spun away, giggling.

"I'll see to it that you regret that. Just wait till I get my cane." He brandished an imaginary weapon as he led the weary Melissa away.

Debbie sank down on the sofa, her feet straight out in front of her. She didn't feel as if she were flying now. Why couldn't she hold onto that sense of freedom?

There was no telling how long she might have sat there had the phone not rung. All the way to the kitchen Debbie found herself trying to move by pushing and gliding as if still on wheels. But when the brief conversation was over, her sensation was not one of skating or of flying, but of sinking.

The minute she recognized the voice of Rachael, manager of Rainbow Land in Boise, she had a premonition. "I'm terribly sorry, Debbie. I know how much you were counting on this job. And you'd have been perfect for it. But Micron isn't transferring Rita's husband after all. So we won't have a job opening."

Debbie didn't reply, so Rachael continued. "But we want to be fair. We'll pay for the month's deposit you mentioned putting on an apartment here if you want to look elsewhere since the job market is a bit depressed here right now. Er—I know this isn't exactly what you had in mind, but I called our Portland store. They do have an opening for a salesgirl. You might be able to work up to designing and teaching."

Debbie was so numb she could hardly write down the directions Rachael dictated. "OK. Yes. Can you repeat that phone number?" she made scratches on the pad. "Sure. Thanks, Rachael. I understand. I'll be OK."

Rachael repeated her apologies and good wishes, but Debbie didn't really listen. The idea was shattering. Give up her apartment? Take a job in Portland? But what about Angie and her baby? What about Andy and his college? These kids had problems. They needed her. She had come to the coast for a little vacation. Just a short break. She had no intention of *moving*. She couldn't leave them to live more than 400 miles away. Suppose . . . Suppose . . . She couldn't even put a name to the crises that might occur.

Well, one thing was certain. There was no way she was going to abandon them like her mother had abandoned her. She— She— But Debbie couldn't think what she could do.

Yet she was all too aware of the depressing job situation Rachael had alluded to. Her movements stiff and jerky, Debbie picked up the phone and called the number she had scrawled on the pad. She tentatively made an appointment to go in for an interview next week. After all, she could always cancel it. The whole idea made her feel sick at her stomach.

The receiver lowered of its own weight. Then she snatched it up again as it touched the cradle. She would call that woman back right now. What a silly idea to think she could leave the twins. Her finger raced to push the buttons. "I just realized I can't make it." That was all she needed to say.

The irritating beep of a busy line greeted her. Well, she could call back in a minute.

Debbie was still sitting, staring at the phone when Melissa, bright-eyed from her short nap, appeared at the door in a lemon yellow dress with a big white collar framing her elfin face. She carried her teddy bear apron and a yellow hair bow, which she held out to Debbie. "They never stay right when Daddy puts them in."

Debbie picked up several strands of the shining silken hair, twisted it into a tiny knot, and pinned the bow securely through it. Melissa shook her head experimentally. "It stayed! How'd you do that?"

"Magic. I'll show your dad how to do it for you." They turned their attentions to making the miniature quiche lorraine tarts Debbie had decided on for an appetizer. Melissa filled the little fluted pastry shells with crumbles of crisp bacon and grated sharp cheese, then Debbie poured in a custardy mixture of eggs and milk.

They moved the table from the kitchen to the living room so they could eat with a view of the ocean. Debbie let Melissa arrange the candles and the gift on the table while she ran out to cut a bowlful of small, red roses from the bush climbing up the south side of the cottage. There weren't many in flower right now, so she added the best blooms from the bouquet she had arranged several days ago, recutting the stems under running water.

Melissa observed her for a moment. "Why are you doing that?"

"I'm making fresh cuts so the flowers can drink better. They'll stay fresh longer."

"But why are you using old flowers?"

Debbie shrugged. "I always do that when I can. I don't know. Some people throw flowers out the minute they start to droop. I just can't stand to waste anything. It seems that if there's life in anything it should be given a chance. I don't throw anything away until it's really dead." Melissa nodded and turned back to the table. Then an idea hit Debbie. "Melissa, go invite Byrl to our party while I put another plate on."

It would have been hard for Debbie to decide later which gave her more satisfaction: Greg's surprise, Melissa's delight, Byrl's pleasure in being included, or her own pride in the evening's success.

Greg arrived at seven o'clock sharp. Melissa met him at the door and flung herself into his arms yelling, "Surprise, Daddy!"

He looked confused over just what surprise she was alluding to until Debbie stepped into view wiping her hands on a lace-edged Victorian apron. He grinned. "Er, am I to understand there has been a change in plans?"

"No change at all." Debbie led the way to the living room. "We just decided to let the guest of honor in on it, that's all." She lit the tall white tapers that were stuck in glasses of sand because the cottage cupboards yielded no candlesticks. The glow from the flickering candles and the gentle sunset beyond the wide window turned the assorted dishes and glassware into Wedgwood and Waterford. Or was it the spirit of camaraderie that made the transformation?

Melissa proudly passed the tray of bite-sized quiches, explaining how she filled them and drawing rave reviews above the clear, graceful notes of the Mozart horn concerto from Debbie's CD player. When they went to the table the plates of creamy white sole garnished with green grapes and pink shrimp, the bright red tomatoes, the deep green asparagus spears, and the tweedy brown wild rice were equally delectable to eye and palate.

They ate slowly, interspersing each succulent mouthful with light chatter. Although Byrl entered genially, Debbie often felt her cousin withdraw mentally into a far corner as if to observe and contemplate the proceedings. And Debbie knew the times Greg's warm gaze met and held hers didn't go unobserved.

Earlier Debbie had piled her meringue crust high with a filling of melted sweet chocolate folded into whipped cream. Now she lit the five candles Melissa had stuck in the filling. "Happy birthday to you . . ." They all sang while Greg made a great show of huffing and puffing at the candles to entertain his daughter.

"Speech, speech!" Debbie and Byrl demanded.

"I've been working on that," Greg said with a slow smile. "But I think I'll save it for later. Large audiences give me cold feet."

"What is this, your contracts limit your television audiences to no more than a hundred thousand at a time or something?" Byrl asked.

"Depends on the speech."

"Open your present now, Daddy!" Melissa pointed to the box that had held the center of the table all through the meal.

Melissa held her breath and bit her lip in excitement while Greg prolonged the agony by untying the red ribbon with exaggerated deliberation. Finally the tissue paper fell away. "Oh. It's perfect." Greg held the eagle up to catch the detail of its workmanship in the candlelight.

"It goes with the verse in the Bible." Melissa clapped her hands and bounced up and down on the chair.

"Sure, I remember. But it's really incredible that you do. You're some little lady, Punkin." And he leaned over and kissed his daughter on the cheek.

Byrl finished her swallow of coffee, then jumped up. "Come on, Melissa, let's do the dishes so your dad can take Debbie out on the beach and rehearse his speech. He's *obviously* in need of elocution lessons."

"What's elocution?"

"Come on, I'll explain it to you."

Debbie slipped on her white jacket, but before going out

with Greg she stuck her head in the kitchen. "Now be sure you cover all the leftovers tight with plastic wrap before you put them in the fridge."

Byrl gave her a scathing look. "I've never known anyone so compulsive in all my life. Will you get out of here!"

They went. Their stroll took them up a faintly lit walk. The velvet darkness was broken by the twinkle of a few beach fires, a sprinkling of stars peeking around clouds, and an amber glow from the old-fashioned street lamps along the Prom. Greg's arm, warm and secure, guided her to a secluded bench. They sat for a moment, listening to the roll of the breakers that were visible only as a hint of white on the dark horizon. "It's the best birthday I've ever had." Greg's voice was soft and slow, as if he were giving the matter careful consideration.

"See, that means you're getting better, not older."

He took her hand. "I'm hoping that things are going to get incredibly better soon."

The tightness in Debbie's throat and stomach, the pounding in her ears was not at all what such romantic surroundings and Greg's hopeful words were meant to produce. "I hope you'll have a terrific year, Greg. But it seems you just can't count on anything. You know that great teaching and designing job I told you about?"

Greg looked crestfallen that the conversation had taken such a turn, but he listened attentively as Debbie told him about the disappointment of her phone call.

When she mentioned the interview appointment in Portland, though, he broke into a broad smile. "But that's wonderful! I know it's selfish of me to be so happy when it's a lesser job for you. But, Debbie—you'll be in *Portland.* Nothing could be better!"

She pulled away from him. "It isn't the job. Don't you see? I'll be so far away from Angie and Andy. I told you about their problems. I even felt guilty coming away for a vacation. And I was right. Everything is falling apart for them. I need to be there!"

"You're exaggerating, Debbie. They're adults. They have their own lives. Angie has a husband. Your father lives near them. I know you'll miss them, but they'll be fine."

"Fine! They'll be fine! What do you know about it? Do you think I'd just go away—desert them like my mother deserted me? Leave them to make decisions on their own like she left me?" In her agitation Debbie had jumped to her feet and moved to the railing.

Greg crossed the walk to her. He took her shoulder and turned her to him, but remained at arms' length. "Debbie, are you still angry about your mother's death?"

"Well of course I'm angry. What do you expect? She was my mother. And she left. I needed her. And she wasn't there." Hot tears stung her eyes. She pulled away from Greg.

"Yes. Anger is a perfectly normal stage of grief. Denial. Anger. That's what we all feel at the first shock of losing someone we love. But, Debbie, you can't stay there."

"Don't tell me what I'm supposed to feel!"

"I'm sorry. I didn't mean to lecture. I'm trying to help you understand. You don't have to live with this anger. If you let yourself grieve for your mother's death, you can forgive her for leaving you. Then you'll come to acceptance. You'll still miss her. You'll still regret the time you didn't have together. But you won't be angry."

"You don't know anything about it. Forgive her! You expect me to forgive—"

"Oh, *thank goodness! There* you are." They turned at the sound of Byrl's voice. "I'm *so* sorry to interrupt, but I didn't know what to do."

"What is it?" Greg asked.

"I tried to comfort her, but I'm afraid Auntie Byrl just doesn't have the magic touch. I was so afraid you'd be out on the beach, and I'd *never* find you."

"Byrl, what happened?" Greg's voice was tight with apprehension.

"Melissa. She has a terrible tummyache. I expect she just

ate too much dinner, but I didn't know what to do."

Debbie almost had to jog to keep up with Greg's long stride. When they reached the cottage she made no attempt to follow him across the room to the sofa. Melissa lay curled in a small bundle of misery, her hand on her tummy, making tiny whimpering sounds. Debbie pushed herself against the wall, gripping her own abdomen, fighting for control of her emotions.

Melissa looked up and gave her daddy a flicker of a smile. "Where's Debbie?"

"She's right here, Punkin." His look commanded Debbie across the room.

She moved jerkily to the sofa. "It was an awfully rich meal for a child, and she was so excited—and after all the exercise earlier. It could just be indigestion." Debbie forced herself to lay a hand on the little forehead. "She's hot, but not burning. It could be the flu or something. Not knowing what to do is the hardest part of raising children."

"Do you think I should give her anything?"

Debbie considered for a moment. "If it's indigestion she'd probably just throw it up. The twins' pediatrician always recommended ice packs. Let's try that. If the pain continues, we'd better call a doctor. Do you have a doctor here?"

Greg shook his head.

Debbie turned toward the kitchen. She returned with a plastic bag of ice wrapped in a soft cloth. Melissa was moaning and tossing on the sofa. Greg knelt beside her, a look of defenseless agony on his face. "Where does it hurt, honey?" Debbie asked. Melissa put her hand just to the left of her stomach. Debbie placed the ice pack there very gently. "Now I'm going to give you a little piece of ice to suck. Don't chew it or swallow it whole, OK?"

In a few minutes the restless tossing stopped, and Melissa seemed easier. Debbie felt her forehead. "She feels cooler. I think we should get her to bed."

"I'm going to carry you home. OK, Punkin?"

Melissa nodded and gave her daddy a weak smile. "Debbie come too."

Debbie grabbed a light blanket to protect Melissa from the night air. Byrl held the door for them. Together Debbie and Greg got Melissa into a pair of soft flannel pajamas and Greg gave her a teddy to hug while Debbie rearranged the ice pack. Debbie leaned over to kiss her good night. "Aren't you going to tell me Peter Rabbit?"

"Of course I will." Debbie sat in the chair Greg pulled up to the bedside for her. ". . . 'now my dears, you may go into the fields or down the lane. But be sure you don't go into Mr. McGregor's garden. Your father had an accident there. He was put into a pie by Mrs. McGregor' . . ."

By the time she got to, ". . . 'He lost one of his shoes among the cabbages, and the other shoe amongst the potatoes,'" Melissa's relaxed, even breathing told them she was asleep. Greg snapped on a nightlight, and they tiptoed from the room.

"Do you think I should stay?" Debbie was still looking back at the half-closed door. "I'd be glad to if you think she might need anything in the night. Really, I—"

Greg shook his head. "My room is just across the hall. I'll leave our doors open."

"But she might need . . . I—"

"Debbie, you don't have to be responsible for everybody. You aren't abandoning anyone. Melissa will be fine with me. Just like Angela will be fine with her husband . . ."

She didn't want to hear any more. She ran from the cottage, straight to her room and slammed the door. What did he know? What did anyone know? Her mother knew. Of course she did. Mothers knew everything. And Debbie knew too—sometimes. But if she said *No* firmly enough it was as if it hadn't happened. Just deny it. That was the trick. But she couldn't always deny the pain.

And he could never forgive. Some things could never be forgiven.

Chapter 13

By noon the next day Debbie was still seething over Greg's attitude the night before. That he should presume to tell her how she should react to things. He didn't even know how she felt about his own daughter, much less how she felt about her sister or mother. But then, Debbie didn't really know how she felt about Melissa, either. Sometimes she felt as if the child were her own. But at other times she felt almost desperate to draw back from the clinging needs of the youngster. The demands of motherhood were so—so *demanding.* So constant.

And not always fulfilling. Raising Angela had taught her that. She had tried to pour herself into her sister, to nurture her in every possible way. But the attempt had left Debbie feeling barren.

And now there was Melissa. And she knew that in the end, any attempt at nurturing Melissa would leave her unfulfilled as well. Because Debbie knew she didn't have a right to love Melissa.

It took several attempts of Byrl's exaggerated rattling the newspaper for Debbie to shift her attention back to the lunch table. "Oh, did you say something?"

Byrl held out the paper. "Big hoo-hah in the paper. Citizen's group up in arms about plans to build a casino in Seaside."

Debbie looked at the photo of an attractive woman with short dark hair addressing a large crowd. "Oh, that's Margaret Larsen."

"You sound like you know her."

"Well, not exactly. I just feel like I know her since I was

on the beach when her husband died." She returned to the article. . . . *Mrs. Larsen charged that fraud had taken place in high circles two years ago . . . vowed to disclose the cover-up . . .* "That's really great that she's carrying on her husband's work. What a memorial." She finished the column and put the paper down.

"Interesting, isn't it?" Byrl said. "Seems no one would have known anything at all about the deal if some clerk hadn't let the monkey out of the bag when Mrs. Larsen was cleaning out her husband's office. Apparently the approval for the whole scheme was supposed to have been granted entirely on the QT, but Larsen thought the citizenry should vote on it."

Byrl tapped a pencil on the table. "If anyone asked me, I'd say money changed hands under the table . . ."

Debbie blinked, trying to recall what that reminded her of. Probably some TV show, she decided with a shrug. "You know, Byrl, it sounds like Mrs. Larsen could use someone with your knowledge of effective assertiveness to help in her campaign."

"She probably could. Not sure I'd have time, though. When deadlines start looming I'm always reminded why they call them *dead*lines."

"Hm?"

"Because either you kill yourself trying to meet them, or you're dead if you don't."

Debbie returned to the front page news. "Byrl! Did you see this next article?"

"No, I didn't get the paper back."

"Oh, sorry. But listen. 'The license was to be granted to Ryburg corporation, Ryland Carlsburg, President.' I don't believe it. He told me all about his plans for a luxury hotel and the trouble he was having getting a permit. But that was all about environmental impact . . ."

"And a huge casino on the beach *wouldn't* impact the environment?"

"It certainly would. But don't you see? He was lying to me all the time—or at least only telling me part of the truth. I can't believe it." Now she remembered what Byrl's assumptions reminded her of—that whispered conversation she overheard on the beach. Could they have been referring to the Ryburg project? Debbie's hands felt cold.

Now that she knew Ryburg was involved she looked again at the account of Margaret Larsen's charges: Cover-up of fraud in high places—two years ago— *When Gayle Mansfield was working in Salem? Who was covering up what?*

The telephone rang, and Byrl reached for it. "Well, *hello*. You're famous this morning. Or should I say notorious? . . . Debbie? . . . Well, I suppose, but I'm not so sure she wants to talk to you—or that you want to hear what's on her mind if she does . . ." She held out the receiver to Debbie. "He says he'll take his chances."

Debbie took the phone. "Ryland? What—"

His voice was smooth and warm, with just a touch of humor. How could it sound so good to her when she was so mad at him?

"No, I really don't think—" He wouldn't listen to her protests. And she supposed it would only be fair to allow him to explain in person. "Well, I don't think there's any chance you'll change my mind. But I guess we could have lunch. . . . Yeah, OK. Call me when you get to town. . . . Sure, I'll still be here at the end of the week. . . . Talk to anyone? Who would I talk to? . . . Don't be silly. I'm not political."

After he'd rung off she sat there, frowning. "Why would he think I'd talk to Margaret Larsen? What would I say to her?"

Byrl pushed her chair back with a scrape. "Well, I don't know about you. But I've got a thing or two to say. It suddenly occurred to me that helping Mrs. Larsen defeat Ryburg would be a great way to get back at that snake Alex. If there was any under-the-table dealing, it's certain he was the bag man."

"That's great. You'll be a big help to her. But, Byrl—"

"Hm?"

"Be careful."

"What do you mean?"

"I don't know. But there's a lot of money at stake. These people might play pretty rough."

Byrl just laughed as she went out.

As she washed dishes Debbie wondered how Melissa was feeling. She would just give the cottage a quick cleaning, then go find out. As she got into the job, however, it seemed that there could be no such thing as a quick cleaning. Debbie hadn't realized how she'd let things slip. How long had it been since she'd given the place a good turnout? She couldn't really remember. And the way sand tracked in around here . . . How could she have put up with this? She must have been more distracted by Greg than she realized to have let her work go like this.

It was hours later before the entire cottage gleamed with waxed floors, shampooed carpets, washed windows . . . Debbie was deep in the hall closet, just thinking she really should pull everything out to get it absolutely immaculate, when she heard a distant jangling. She jerked up and turned quickly, knocking against a shelf. The ringing sounded above the clatter of falling boxes. Yes, it was the phone. "Don't hang up, I'm coming." But her attempt to hop over the jumble brought the real disaster. She bumped into the ironing board, knocking it firmly across the doorway.

She pushed at it in frustration, only lodging it more firmly against the doorframe. "Hold on." But the phone went silent. With a sigh of exasperation Debbie turned to straighten the chaos she had created. Was that Greg reporting on Melissa? What if the child was worse and they needed her? Well, she'd just finish this quickly, then call them.

She was just closing the door on her completed job when the phone rang again. This time there were no barriers. "Hello, Greg?"

"Er—no. Who's Greg? Something going on there I don't know about?"

"Andy! Is that you? What's wrong?"

"Nothing's wrong. That's what I called to tell you. But who's Greg?"

"He's a friend. A neighbor." No one. Everyone. She didn't really know. "But tell me about you. How are you?"

"I'm great. That's what I called to tell you. I'm going back to school."

"Oh, that is great! What changed your mind?"

"I didn't really change my mind. The job was just an excuse. But I knew there was no use going on with school unless I was going to do it right. Registration is next week, so I had to get it settled."

"What?"

"My call to be a missionary. You remember, don't you? I talked about it a lot when I was a kid. Well, it never changed. But I got cold feet, especially when Mom died and all that."

"Yeah. I know. Mothers who desert their families have a lot to answer for."

"What? Deb, you don't mean that. Mom didn't desert us. She died praying for us. I don't know—maybe she's still praying for us."

Debbie was silent.

"Sis? Are you there?"

"I'm here."

"You didn't mean that did you? About Mom deserting us? You make it sound like she had a choice. She didn't choose to die."

Silence.

"Deb. You know what I'm saying is right."

"My head knows. I still feel . . . I don't know. Abandoned. Betrayed. Forced to do things I didn't want to do."

"You mean like taking care of Angie and me? I know we must have been a pain, especially me, but—"

"No, Andy. That isn't at all what I mean. I don't know

what I mean. Anyway, I'm glad you've got your future sorted out. Really glad."

"Yeah, me too. But, Deb, what about you? I mean, do you have anyone there you can talk to? You need to get your feelings—"

"Now don't you start too. My feelings are just that. Mine. I don't need anyone else telling me what to feel and not to feel."

She hadn't meant to hang up on him. She was really glad, so very glad for Andy. She knew his decision was right. But the fact that he almost missed it, that their mother's death almost derailed him, too, just added fuel to the fire of her emotions. She had thought she would go see Melissa, but she didn't want to see anyone right now. Besides, she really must finish her work here.

She looked around. How could this place feel so grubby when she had just spent hours cleaning? Oh, that was it. The kitchen cupboards. She would pull everything out, scrub the shelves, wash the contents, put in new shelf paper. Then they would be clean. Then she would feel better.

Byrl came in some time later and began digging in the newly cleaned refrigerator filled with freshness-sealed leftovers. She pulled out a dish and turned to the microwave while she enthused about her meeting with Margaret Larsen, about what a brave, dynamic woman she was, about how Byrl was going to write all the press releases for her campaign to run the casino gambling interests out of Oregon. Debbie nodded at appropriate intervals, but she wasn't really concentrating.

She simply had far too much work to do here to think about anything else. And she hadn't touched the bathroom yet. She would probably have to run to the store for a good strong disinfectant. Molds and things could really take hold in a damp climate like this. Thank goodness she'd done Byrl's room when she had the chance. She heard her cousin's door shut and knew she wouldn't see her for hours—probably not until morning—once she got into her writing.

It was dark out. Debbie's back ached. Her hands were raw. But at last she felt calm inside. Whatever she had been trying to scrub away was now safely tidied up. For the moment. She knew from experience that the compulsion to clean and clean and clean would stay quietly buried now until something else triggered it. She didn't understand what it was or why it happened. She just knew that was the way of it.

There was only one thing left. Now she must clean herself. A hot bath. Wash her hair. Scrub her face. But most of all her hands. She was desperate to wash her hands. She almost ran to the sink, filled it with hot water, grabbed the bar of soap and ran it around and around and around in her hands. Lather bubbled through her fingers and dripped off her elbows. But she didn't stop.

"What are you doing?" Byrl's voice made her jump.

"There's so much blood." It wasn't Debbie's voice. She couldn't have said that.

Byrl just stood there, looking at her, frowning. "'Aye, there's a spot. And another.' Lady Macbeth." She walked away, shaking her head.

Byrl's words jarred Debbie awake. No, she'd been awake. Just thinking about other things. Lady Macbeth? What did she mean by that? Lady Macbeth was a murderer. Of course she had blood on her hands. She had killed. With her own hands. Why did Byrl say that? What did she know? But that was silly. There wasn't anything to know. Debbie hadn't killed anyone. Of course she hadn't.

The house was dirty. She had cleaned it. The cleaning chemicals made her hands sore. She washed them off. What was the big deal about that? She would just finish her bath and then run over and see how Melissa was. She'd meant to do that hours ago.

But she didn't calculate for dozing off in the tub. When she emerged from the bath it really was too late to go running next door. She would just eat an egg and some toast and go to bed. She could check on Melissa in the morning. Before leaving the kitchen, however, she pushed back the curtains and opened the window for a breath of fresh air. Fog was rolling in from the ocean, but she could see the light on in the cottage next door. If Greg was awake, she might as well give him a call to tell him about Andy.

The phone rang three times. She was just ready to hang up when Greg answered. He sounded amazed to hear her voice. "Debbie, how could you have known? I considered calling, but didn't want to disturb you."

"Know what? I called to tell you about Andy."

"Andy?"

"My brother. You prayed for him."

"Oh, yeah. Sorry."

Greg sounded distracted, but she went on. "Andy called. He's going back to college. It wasn't the school or his job. He was fighting a call to the mission field."

"Yep."

"You sound like you knew that."

"I was pretty sure."

"How?"

"Went through it myself. Not missions—preaching. Listen, that's great about Andy, I want to hear all about it. But I've got another problem here."

"What? It is Melissa? I'm sorry. I should have come over earlier. Is she sick?"

"I don't know, maybe. I went in to her because she was thrashing around. She's calm now, but—"

"What?"

"Debbie, this isn't easy to tell you. I found your compact."

"My compact! Where?"

"Under Melissa's pillow."

"How'd it get there?"

"I don't want to go into it all now, but there were problems before. She seemed so well this summer, especially af-

ter you came into our life. I thought— I really don't know."
He sounded despondent.

"Shall I come over? It isn't important about the compact. Tell her she can have it. No, wait, I'll tell her myself."

"No. Don't come now. She's asleep. I just don't know what to do."

"Greg, don't worry. She's only a child. She doesn't understand about stealing."

"I know that. It isn't the fact of taking the stuff. It's the need for security that the things symbolize. It hadn't happened all summer. I thought—"

"Greg, are you sure you don't want me to come over?"

"Yeah, I'm sure. I'm going to try to get some sleep too."

Debbie glanced at her clock as she got into bed. No wonder Greg didn't want her to come over. How could it possibly be so late?

The next time the phone rang Debbie didn't even look at her clock. She didn't want to know what time it was. She might have slept for two hours, but it seemed like two minutes. All she knew was that it was still dark outside. And her head ached abominably.

"Debbie, I'm sorry to bother you, but we're at the hospital, and Melissa is asking for you. Could you possibly—?"

"Hospital?" she was as instantly awake as if she had been doused with a pitcher of cold water.

"Melissa woke up screaming about half an hour ago. They're running some tests, but the doctor's pretty sure it's appendicitis. He says it's unusual in a child her age, but . . ."

Debbie's hands were icy. Perspiration stood out on her forehead. "Hospital?"

"I'm so sorry to bother you. I wouldn't, except she really wants you. And I explained about her insecurities. Well, I didn't exactly explain, but she really needs you."

Debbie's throat was closing. The room going dark. She leaned against the wall to keep from falling.

"Debbie, are you there? What shall I tell Melissa?"

She fought her way up as if from a long distance. Tell Melissa? About going to the hospital? She hadn't even gone to the hospital when . . .

"Debbie?"

"Yeah, I'm here." She cleared her throat and spoke louder. "Tell her I'm coming."

"Do you know the way?"

"Oh, I hadn't thought of that. Tell me." She fumbled for paper and pencil.

He gave her the address. It was some Indian name she had never heard before and didn't know how to spell. "Take the highway toward Cannon Beach. About four blocks past the junction turn toward the mountains. The road twists around, but there's nothing else there, so you can't miss it. It's in the woods, but you'll see the lights. I'd come for you, but I hate to leave Melissa."

"No. No, don't leave her. I'll find it."

Groping in the semidarkness she pulled on jeans and a sweater, awkward in her haste. She jammed her feet into a pair of sneakers. She was almost out the door when she thought of her hair. She turned back to splash cold water on her face and run a brush through her sleep-tangled mane. All the while she knew she should be praying. She tried. Tried to pray for Melissa, for herself, for Greg, for the doctors. But no words came. She tried to raise her mind upward but hit only a black ceiling.

A solid wall of cold, wet fog engulfed her outside the door. This was something she could pray about. *Don't let me get lost in this.* It was too dark to drive without lights, yet the fog just threw them back at her eyes. She drove more by instinct than by sight to the highway, hoping that even a few blocks back from the ocean the fog might be thinner. But if anything, it piled up more thickly at the base of the mountains. *Help me! Please.*

A red light suddenly loomed before her. She threw on her brake and skidded into the intersection. At least she knew she was at Broadway now. Silly to have streetlights going at this hour. She was the only soul awake in the whole town. Could be the only one alive for all she could see. "Turn at the junction," he had said.

Then with horror she realized she didn't know *which* junction—the one at the edge of town or the one out on the highway? She searched her mind to recall Greg's words, something about the highway toward Cannon Beach. Both junctions qualified. It sounded so simple when he said it. Her hands gripped the steering wheel, stiff with the penetrating cold. Her headache returned. *Just get me there.*

She counted four streets past the first junction and turned to the left, even afraid to breathe as she did so. If this was the wrong choice, she could drive for an hour in the forest and never find anything. She considered getting out and searching for a sign. If this was the way to the hospital, it must be marked. But she didn't have a flashlight. Finding a sign in almost zero visibility seemed hopeless.

Better just to keep on. She realized she was holding her breath and forced herself to breathe. Slow, deep breaths to calm herself. No. That was what they had told her to do . . . No. NO. She shook her head. No. She wouldn't think of that. She gulped air in rapidly.

If only the engine would warm up, so she could turn on the heater. Her feet were numb all the way to her knees. She had been cold like that— No, stop that. She looked at the heater gauge. It still registered below cold. *Are You there, God? I need You.*

All at once her headlights caught the trunks of heavy, dark pine trees right in front of her. Was this the end of the road? She threw on her brakes. What now? There wasn't even a turnaround. Then, as her eyes probed the fuzzy darkness, she realized the road hadn't ended. It turned sharply left.

Her attention riveted on the road ahead, driving almost by Braille, she crept down the road, aware that thick forest surrounded her on either side. She was encased in mist and uncertainty. Surely no one would build a hospital in such a remote place. Greg must have meant the second junction. And now she'd be too late. Melissa would go to surgery without her. She hadn't meant to abandon Melissa.

She hadn't meant to. She'd fought as hard as she could. She didn't want Melissa to have to go through that alone. Not without a mother. Debbie knew how that felt. Mothers should be there when they were needed.

Then a dim flicker of light appeared through the murk. It seemed like hours since she'd seen any sign of civilization. It couldn't really have been more than a matter of minutes— 15, maybe. But it seemed a lifetime. Leading her like a beacon, the single light became two. Then three. Then, with a shout of joy, Debbie turned in at a brightly lit, efficient-looking brick building clearly marked Hospital. *Thank you.*

Greg was standing just inside the glass doors watching for her. He held the doors open. She ran into his arms. For a moment she forgot where she was and why she was there.

Greg released her and led the way down the hall. "The fog is awful. I thought I'd never get here. Am I too late? Have they taken her in?"

He replied, but Debbie couldn't focus on his words. The smell hit her first. That awful smell of death. She put her hand over her nose and closed her eyes. A streak of red slashed the inside of her eyelids. A cry.

"Are you all right?" Greg took her arm.

She blinked at him. Where was she? "Yeah, I'm fine. Just a little woozy. I don't like hospitals."

Greg pushed through a swinging door to a white room with a high metal bed in the center. "Just made it." He pointed to the small figure in the bed. "Her blood count is high, abdomen hard. They're going to take her to surgery in about five minutes."

White walls. White sheets. Metal bed. Dim lights. *Let me out of here. I have to get out!* She crossed stiffly to the little figure hardly making a wrinkle in the stiff white sheet. "I'm here, Melissa." She felt under the covers for the tiny hand. It closed tightly on hers.

Then Melissa put her hand on her abdomen and whimpered. Debbie wanted to grab her own stomach. She wanted to yell at the universe to stop. This couldn't be happening.

Melissa opened her eyes and gave Debbie a weak smile. "Don't go away."

Concentrate. Act like everything is fine. The way you've always done. "Don't worry, darling. I'll be here all the time."

"Promise?"

"Cross-cross applesauce."

Melissa smiled, then closed her eyes.

"She's pretty heavily sedated," Greg said.

Debbie was still standing there holding Melissa's hand when the orderly came in. Crisp white uniform with scrubs over it. Swift, businesslike movements that put up the side railing and wheeled the bed from the room.

Debbie felt the motion. "No, wait, stop. I don't want to. I've changed my mind. No. No."

Greg put his arm around her. She fought. She would have screamed, but she choked on the sound.

Debbie's sobs were muffled as Greg pressed her against his shoulder. "Debbie, it's all right. You're safe."

She looked up, surveying the room. They were alone. She and Greg. She was standing here in the middle of the room. She wasn't on that gurney being wheeled into surgery. It wasn't that at all. Why had she thought . . . ? Was she really going crazy?

Greg put his hands on her shoulders and held her steady. His eyes commanded her attention. "Debbie, that wasn't about Melissa, was it?"

She shook her head.

"We need to talk about this." He steered her to a stiff, chrome and plastic chair.

"Not here. I don't want to talk here. I can't breathe in here."

"Debbie." His hand on her shoulder still held her. "You can't run away forever. Going to the coffee shop or some-place outside won't really change anything, will it?"

Again, she shook her head.

He took a chair next to hers and turned to face her. "Is it your mother?"

"Yes. Yes, of course it's my mother! What did you think it was? What else could it be?"

"Your mother died in the hospital."

"Yes."

"Tell me about it."

"She had cancer. I was a senior in high school. She had been sick for several months—in a lot of pain. The doctor told us from the first that she was terminal."

"No, I mean about when she died."

"I told you. It was November. She'd been in the hospital for two weeks."

"Tell me about the last day. The last hours."

"She was in pain. She wouldn't take much medication because she wanted to recognize her family. She died about midnight."

"Tell me about her room. What it looked like."

"All hospital rooms look alike. Four white walls. It was a private room."

"Were there flowers?"

"Sure."

"Pictures on the wall?"

"I don't know."

"Debbie. Close your eyes and tell me what you see. Tell me about it."

"Green walls. On a gurney. Going down a long hall. Green walls with pictures. Dogs and trees. *No, wait. Stop. I don't want to. I've changed my mind!*"

"What have you changed your mind about?"

"I don't want an abortion!"

Chapter 14

Debbie looked at him as the words echoed around the empty room. . . . *Abortion. I don't want an abortion. Stop! I don't want . . .*

She was stiff. Cold. Where had those words come from?

"You were never in your mother's hospital room, were you?"

"I couldn't. I couldn't go. This is the first time I've been in a hospital since—"

"Since the abortion?"

She shook her head. "It was her fault. I couldn't see her again. I wanted her to die. She had killed my baby. I wanted her to die too." Debbie had a vague feeling that she should be sobbing or yelling—showing some emotion. But the words came out hard and dry. Staccato. Detached.

"When you discovered you were pregnant after being with Shawn, your mother told you to get an abortion?"

"No, of course not. You don't think I *told* her, do you? She was dying. I had to take care of everything myself. All on my own. I didn't even have a friend to go with me. I couldn't let anyone know. I had to protect them all. They had more than they could cope with. I couldn't upset them more. No one knew. No one ever had the slightest suspicion."

"But you knew. And you could never get away from it."

"What do you mean?" Her words were a challenge. What was he accusing her of now?

"Your nightmares. The broken babies—dolls, I mean."

She shook her head. "They were babies. I see now. I always knew. Sort of. I knew it had happened, and yet I didn't. I didn't have amnesia or anything. I just stuffed the memory down so far I couldn't see it."

161

"But you felt it." Greg's voice was the most soothing sound she had ever heard.

Now the tears came. "All those broken babies. But I told myself it couldn't have been the abortion. The counselor at the clinic said I might be a little depressed, but that there wouldn't be any real problem. She said women always felt better after an abortion. It was good for them to have the freedom to choose. It would make my life better. It couldn't have caused my problems. It would enhance my self-esteem—taking control of my own life. The counselor said it over and over."

"Did you believe her?"

"I wanted to. I thought I did. Until I was strapped on the table. Then I fought and cried and screamed. But it was too late. The nurse said I was just upset. That there was nothing to be afraid of. That I'd be glad when it was over. That I'd forget all about it."

Tears were running down her cheeks, but she wasn't sobbing. Greg handed her a soft white handkerchief. "I tried everything to forget. I told myself that if I just worked harder it would all go away like it was supposed to. And sometimes it did. Sometimes I didn't think about it for weeks—months. I thought about the rape and about my mother's death. But not about the other. It was normal to be upset about those things. It wasn't normal to be upset by an abortion. They said I wouldn't be."

"Did you write to Shawn like we talked about?"

"I tried."

"Did it help?"

"Not much. I thought it would, but . . . I didn't mail the letter."

"Do you have any idea why it didn't help?"

She nodded. "Because . . ." She dropped her head. "Because I didn't really forgive him. I wrote the words, but I didn't mean them." She sniffed and dabbed at her eyes. "It's strange, but I don't think I really connected the two. I mean,

I blamed him for—for violating me. But I didn't see that he had done far less damage to me than I did to my baby." Now the sobs came.

"I never kill anything. Not even bugs or weeds. I never waste anything. But I killed a baby. I wasted a human life." Greg pulled her into his arms and held her while she shook with weeping.

She dabbed at the tears streaming down her face. "Oh, this is silly."

Greg continued to hold her. "No it isn't. It's a God-designed process. The tears wash away the pain of your loss. They should have come six years ago, but they were blocked by anger at your mother and guilt over the loss of your child. Let all those tears that have been dammed up for so long come out."

He was still holding her some time later when the surgeon came in wearing his cap and shoe covers. "Mr. Masefield?" He held out his hand. "I'm Dr. Thomas. Your daughter's fine." Debbie closed her eyes in relief. *Thank you.* She had harbored some undefined fear that Melissa would be taken away from her as punishment.

The doctor continued his explanation to Greg, "There were no complications. We didn't have to do any draining. We'll keep her in the recovery room about an hour just so we can watch her, but she'll start to wake up soon. With a young child we don't put them under very deep—just enough to take them to happyland and keep them from wiggling. You can go to her any time now."

"When can she go home?" Greg asked.

"Probably tomorrow. I'll be in to see her later today, so the nurse can tell you for sure this evening."

"Thank you, Doctor." The men shook hands again, and the surgeon disappeared through the swinging doors.

Debbie went to the sink across the room and splashed cold water on her face. It didn't do much for the redness around her eyes, but it felt good. She followed Greg down the hall. A nurse showed them to a room with space for three beds, the curtains partially drawn on the track around the nearest station. "When she wakens she'll be thirsty. Just give her a chip of ice to suck. Don't let her drink anything or it'll upset her stomach." The nurse left them, and Greg pulled two chairs to the bedside.

An aluminum rail ran around the bed like a fence, fluid dripped into Melissa's arm from a tube running to a bottle on a bracket. The little body lay perfectly still, but her breathing seemed normal. Debbie smoothed the blond hair away from the small forehead. She was almost exactly the age that other baby would have been now. Had it been a boy or girl? What would it have looked like? This was the first time Debbie had allowed herself to consider such questions. For six years she had turned her back on small children and pregnant women. She had shut out any reminder of her pain. Now she had opened the wound.

It hurt even worse than she had feared. The tears started again, but silently. They slid out the corners of her eyes and rolled down her face so gently that she wasn't aware of them until one landed on the sheet by Melissa's cheek. Greg, who had probably slept about half an hour in the last 24, leaned forward, his head nestled in his folded arms on the bed. Instantly his heavy breathing told Debbie he was asleep. The room was silent. She was alone with herself.

And for the first time in six years it was safe to be alone without any project or activity to keep herself from thinking. Now she wanted to think. She wanted to think about her mother, especially to recall the good times they had had. She wanted to think about Shawn and hope he had found happiness. She wanted to think about the baby that would never be.

But that was the impossible part. She had admitted what she had done. She had accepted responsibility for having made the decision herself. But she couldn't really think any farther. She was sure there was more she needed to do. She certainly didn't feel the matter was resolved. But the pain was too overwhelming to deal with. And it frightened her. She knew that if she didn't go on to whatever else must be done, she would stay frozen at this new stage. And now that she'd started she could accept nothing but complete healing. She couldn't go back to the way things were before. But how could she go forward?

Less than half an hour later Debbie put her hand on Greg's shoulder and shook him gently. "She's starting to stir. I'll be back in a minute."

Debbie spent only a few minutes in the ladies' room. But when she returned Melissa was awake with a nurse bending over her taking her blood pressure and temperature. Debbie stayed back out of the way. Melissa tossed her head restlessly and spoke around the thermometer. "Where is she?"

The nurse pulled the thermometer from the child's mouth. "Your mother? She's right over there, honey. Now just be still and let me check this, then you can have your mama." No one bothered to correct her.

As soon as the nurse left, Debbie took her place by the bedside. "You said you wouldn't leave," Melissa accused.

"I was just across the hall, honey."

"Don't go away. Ever." Melissa clung to her hand. "Ever. Promise."

Debbie looked around wildly. She felt trapped. What could she say that wouldn't make the situation worse? She didn't want to promise something she couldn't fulfill. "I will always love you. I'll always be with you in my heart." Would a child understand that?

Whether she understood or whether it was merely the lingering effects of the anesthetic, the small hand gripping Debbie's relaxed, and Melissa's breath came soft and rhythmically. The pressure of Greg's hand on her arm pulled Debbie into the hall. "Be careful what you say. She can't take any more broken promises. I told you about the compact."

"I would never promise Melissa or anyone else something I didn't intend to fulfill. I was trying to make it clear to her."

"I know. I'm sorry." He let go of her arm and ran his fingers through his disheveled hair. "I'm overly protective. But after—" He shook his head. "I can't take a chance on her being hurt."

"You're exhausted. Go get some sleep. I'll stay with her."

He hesitated. Debbie held her breath. Was this some kind of test? If so, was it testing him or her? His willingness to trust his child to a woman who had had an abortion? Or her trustworthiness to stay with Melissa?

Whatever caused his doubt, it was probably fatigue that made the decision. "You're sure you don't mind—staying?"

"I wouldn't consider anything else. Now run along. Oh, and give Byrl a ring and tell her about Melissa. I didn't even leave a note last night."

"Sure. And thanks."

"Go." She pointed to the door. "And don't come back until you're coherent."

*　　*　　*

". . . Peter gave himself up for lost. Big tears rolled from his eyes. His sobs were overheard by some friendly sparrows. They flew to him chirping in excitement, and implored him to exert himself . . ."

"Daddy!" Melissa looked toward the door of the hospital room and held out her arms.

Debbie, who was sitting with her back to the door, swung around. The sight of him standing there made her catch her breath. Why was it always a surprise when she saw him? She knew what he looked like, yet there it was, all over again, the amazement that any man could really look that good.

He was leaning with one shoulder against the doorframe, his arms folded over a lightweight green sweater, the collar of a white shirt framing his bronze head. "How long have you been there?" Debbie asked.

"Just since 'round the end of a cucumber frame.'" He pushed away from the door and went to Melissa, returning her hug. "How're you feeling, Punkin?"

"A little ouchy." She placed her hand on her incision. "And all I can eat is Jell-O and chicken soup."

"Awful, isn't it?" he perched on the edge of her bed, his long legs still reaching the floor. "Shall I complain to the management?" Melissa just giggled. He turned to Debbie. "I didn't mean to interrupt your story. I want to hear the end too."

Debbie continued. "Suddenly, quite near him, Peter heard the noise of a hoe. *Scr-r-ritch, scratch, scratch, scritch . . .*"

A nurse breezed in, stuck a thermometer under Melissa's tongue, and held her wrist for a pulse count. When she extracted the thermometer she produced a little white pill and a glass of water. "Now, young lady, Dr. Thomas wants you to have a nice, cozy nap so you can be all bright-eyed when he comes to visit you this afternoon." Melissa swallowed the pill obediently. The nurse pulled the blanket up to her chin. "Your mama and daddy can come back in about two hours."

The nurse's tone said clearly that there was nothing to do but kiss the child good-bye.

"I'll finish the story when I get back," Debbie promised.

"But—"

"We have to mind the doctor, Punkin. Don't worry, I'll bring her back to you." Melissa nodded sleepily. They went out.

"You've been on duty for hours." Greg led the way to the parking lot. "Do you want something to eat? a nap? a bath?"

Debbie shook her head. "The nurse gave me a lunch tray. I just want some fresh air."

As Greg drove out of the woods, Debbie looked in wonder at the world that had seemed so terrifying the night before. Misty remnants of the fog still hung around the dark green trees, but now it gave a feeling of coziness and comfort. And the distance was so short after the torturously slow route of the night before. But then, wasn't that always the way of it? The real terrors were the internal ones.

Greg turned northward toward the uninhabited part of the beach. As usual, he was quiet. Debbie leaned into the plush seat of the car. The road ended in the sand dunes where river and creek came together to run into the ocean. Greg opened her door and helped her out. "Fresh air you wanted. Fresh it is. Will you be cold?"

After hours in the hospital, the cool, moist air felt marvelous on her face. She took a deep breath and held out her arms. "Oh, it's great."

They walked along the peninsula of beach, a few seagulls for their only companions and the surf in the distance the only sound. Debbie realized Greg was even quieter than usual. They walked some distance before he stopped and turned to her. "How do you feel now?"

Debbie watched the roll and retreat of the tide for several moments before she answered. "Battered. Bruised. A little like I did after—after the abortion." It was still so hard to say it. She had to take a breath just to get the word out. "Just as confused. But not as angry. Maybe not as frightened." She considered. "Maybe more frightened."

"You haven't had much time to work through it. It will take time, you know."

"I'm not sure I'll ever be able to forgive myself."

"Have you asked God to forgive you?"

"Every day since— Every day for six years."

"And do you believe He has?"

"My head does. I don't *feel* forgiven."

Greg nodded. "That's because you haven't forgiven yourself."

"But how can I?"

"By accepting God's forgiveness. Trusting that He always does what He says He will do, even if you don't feel anything." He paused. "And don't confuse forgiving and forgetting."

Debbie's head jerked up. "What do you mean?"

"Forgiving is making peace with our mistakes. Accepting what happened and going on from there. But it's important *not* to forget. We need to remember so we can learn from our mistakes."

He put his arm loosely around her shoulder and guided her back to the car. "And remember, in your own human power you can't forgive—even yourself. Just ask God to make you willing to be willing."

All the way home she kept thinking over and over again, *willing to be willing.* Was she willing to forgive herself? To put the terrible decision she had made behind her? To go on from here?

It sounded so good. So easy. She did want to. But was that really enough? Willing to be willing? *Help me.*

Chapter 15

Dr. Thomas released Melissa the next morning. To mark the occasion Debbie brought her the teddy bear in the red flannel pajamas that she had liked so much when they went shopping together. Melissa hugged him all the way home, sitting on Debbie's lap.

Byrl was there to meet them with a bouquet of white daisies and pink rosebuds. They made a great party of tucking Melissa in bed and arranging everything just right for her. "Now, if you're a good girl and rest like the doctor said, I can take you out on the beach in two days," Greg promised. "But no bouncing around, or I'll have to tie you down."

Melissa giggled and lay back against the pillows. "Thank you for the flowers, Auntie Byrl."

"No problem, kid. Just you get better so things will settle down around here and I can get some work done."

"Oh, I will. Mama will take care of me." The little voice was half muffled.

Debbie turned. "What did you say?" She didn't mean for her question to sound sharp, she was just astonished at what she thought she had heard.

"Um, I said 'mama.' Is that all right? The nurse called you that."

"Well, the nurse didn't know us, and it didn't seem worth making a fuss about. But I'm not sure—" Debbie backed a step toward the door. What had she gotten herself into? What in the world would Greg think?

She stopped when she saw Melissa's eyes fill up with tears. "I took your compact."

"Oh, I'd forgotten about that." Now she moved toward the bed. "I know you did. Your daddy found it under your pillow when you were sick." She sat on the edge of the bed. "Do you want to tell me about it?"

Melissa nodded, but no words came out.

"Were you afraid I'd leave and you'd forget me?"

Melissa shook her head. "I thought if you left and I had it you'd have to come back for it."

Debbie took her hand. "How about if we do it the other way around?"

"Hmmm?"

"I'll keep it in my purse. When you want to borrow it, you ask me. OK?"

Melissa smiled and nodded.

Debbie had accepted the nurse's mistaken identity as natural in the circumstances. But how did she feel about this? Her relationship with Greg aside, if he ever asked her to be his wife, how did she feel about Melissa's proposal that she be her mother?

She now understood that this child, no matter how near in age, would never replace her own. She had tried to make Angie and Andy fill that role and had muffed if badly by try- ing to overmanage them. Thank goodness they were strong- minded enough not to let her completely dominate them. But what about Melissa? Could she accept her on a com- pletely different footing? As her own person, not a substitute for someone else?

And what about Debbie's position? Could she fill the role of the deceased mother? She had once felt haunted by Gayle. Would she still? She felt bombarded by questions. And she had no answers. But she knew she must find them if they were all to come through this unscathed.

Melissa's first outing two days later was surrounded with much preparation. The sun was warm and sparkly. Greg put up a large yellow beach umbrella to ward off the breeze. Debbie placed an old quilt over a straw mat and made a nest of pillows for the patient. Greg brought out his cassette player, and after Debbie furnished the portable room with a supply of books, toys, and a teddy bear, Melissa was borne out in her daddy's arms to enjoy it all.

First on the agenda was feeding the seagulls. Debbie had learned when she came to the beach never to throw a crust of bread or crumble of cracker away. She hoarded everything in a brown paper bag marked seagull food. Then enjoyed feeding the local scavengers when the sack was full.

Only one seagull was visible, perched atop one of the streetlights along the Prom. But as soon as Greg attracted its attention with a handful of stale popcorn a whole flock joined it. Debbie propped Melissa in an upright position and let her toss the scraps when the crowd was gathered.

"Toss some to the little one over there." Debbie pointed to a small brown gull. "He hasn't had any yet." Melissa tried, but before he could swallow the kernel a large white bird snatched it out of his beak.

"That's not nice!" Melissa cried.

The supply of crusts ran out, and Melissa lay back against her cushions. The shadow of a newcomer fell across the sand. "Hello. You've got a regular Arabian pleasure tent here, haven't you?"

"Hi, Auntie Byrl." The ready grins between them showed that, whatever reservations Debbie might have about hers, no one had any problem with the honorary title Melissa had bestowed on Byrl.

"What brings you to the surface in the middle of the day?" Debbie asked. "I thought nothing could interrupt your incredible discipline."

"For a workaholic it's taking a break that requires discipline," Byrl replied. "I suddenly realized that we leave here a week from tomorrow, so I told myself that if I didn't get some sand between my toes now, I'd regret it all winter."

Bryl's remark was a jolt to Debbie. She had tried not to count. As long as they could continue with things as they were she didn't have to face the unsolved problems. But even if her mind would let her forget, her calendar wouldn't. This was Friday. Tomorrow was her appointment at Rainbow Land. Greg had even offered to have Courtenay show her available apartments in Portland. Was she ready to cut her ties with the past so definitely?

"Why don't you two go lay in a dune or something, and let me visit with my honorary niece?" Byrl interrupted her reverie. "Want me to read to you?" Byrl looked at the book Melissa was holding.

Melissa considered. "No, I'll just listen to the pictures."

Debbie emerged from under the umbrella and looked around. The beach was never the same twice. Today, under the early afternoon sun, the sand was white, the water dark turquoise and the sky a gentle powder blue. Then a crisp breeze hit her. She hugged her sweatshirt to her. "Lounge on the beach in this wind? Byrl is crazy."

Greg laughed. "You should know by now, it's the only time you get sun here—when there's wind to blow the clouds away. Come on." He led her a short distance from the umbrella to a spot sheltered by a mound of sand. Greg spread two oversized beach towels for them. Debbie pulled off her sweatshirt, spread sunscreen over her arms and legs exposed by the T-shirt and shorts she wore, and wiggled around to hollow out the sand beneath her towel until she had a nest custom made to fit her curves.

On the other side of the dune Byrl changed the tape on the cassette player. The strains of "Victory at Sea" floated to them.

"Ooh, that's great. I think I'll become a beach bum." Debbie relaxed as the sun warmed her face.

Greg stretched out beside her. "And how long would that last?"

"Until the first creative urge struck me. But if I stayed away from fabric shops and cookbooks, I could probably hold off long enough to get a decent tan."

"And then you'd lose it at work."

"Well, in the best of all possible worlds I could move my sewing machine outside."

They were quiet for a while, absorbing the sun and the music. Greg picked up her hand and toyed with her fingers. She opened her eyes lazily, watching him. Then she sat up suddenly and grabbed his hand, spreading it out flat on her knee. She was right. Only a white mark at the base of his fourth finger. His wedding band was gone. "Greg, when did that happen?"

"When I left you alone at the hospital with Melissa."

"Why?"

"Well, you needed reassurance that I trusted you. I thought this might help."

"Because you trusted me or because Melissa needed me?"

He sat up now. The pressure of his hand increased on her knee. "Because we both need you."

She pulled away. "Greg, I can't replace Gayle."

Now he drew back. "Is that what you think? That I want another woman like her?"

"Well, of course." Didn't he? Debbie had tried to make a child take away her pain over losing a baby. Why wouldn't Greg try to do the same thing with a wife?

He was quiet for a long time. At last he spoke. Slowly, quietly, with enormous control. "I should have explained this to you long ago. But it's not easy. It's very hard to admit . . . I'm supposed to be some big Christian speaker and teacher. I'm supposed to be perfect. But I have things that are hard to face too." He took a deep breath. "You need to understand that a great deal of my grief for Gayle was guilt. She was beautiful and intelligent and witty. She was also a very good lawyer. She loved her career. And I was so infatuated with her that I pushed her into a marriage that wasn't right for either of us. Her work always came first. I said that was fine, I understood. But not when we had a child."

He turned now to stare out at the rolling ocean, talking more to himself than to Debbie. "That was my fault too. Gayle should never have been a mother. I think she knew it, but she gave in to me. Then there were three people to hurt instead of two. Time and again she would promise Melissa she'd do something with her. Then the court schedule would change or a client would have an emergency. You've seen the results of that seesaw with Melissa. Of course, Gayle absolutely refused to consider having another child. And she was right."

"Greg." Debbie reached out for his hand.

He took her hand but didn't move any closer to her. "Don't get me wrong. I loved Gayle. Sometimes the loneliness still washes over me." He was quiet for a moment. "I loved her, but we couldn't build the kind of home together that I longed for because that takes teamwork.

"What I'm trying to say is that it takes courage to try again. I won't make the same mistakes. I have learned. But I'm afraid of the new ones I'll make."

Debbie pulled back. He couldn't have been clearer. He had just painted a very vivid picture of what he wanted. A teammate. Working together to build the home and family they both dreamed of. But could she do that?

He stood up suddenly, offering his hand to pull her to her feet. "I'm sorry. I shouldn't have dumped all that on you. I know you weren't ready to hear that yet. Maybe after tomorrow."

Tomorrow? Tomorrow she had those appointments in Portland. What difference would that make to their relationship? Was Greg planning something special?

Chapter 16

The next morning Debbie sat beside Greg as he drove along the curving, wooded highway toward Portland. They had left Melissa happily tucked up in Debbie's bed where Byrl could keep an eye on her and get some work done as well. Although Debbie wondered how much work Byrl would attempt to accomplish. It was amazing the changes she had seen in her cousin this summer. But Byrl wasn't the only one. Debbie's eyes were drawn repeatedly to Greg's ringless left hand.

He glanced over and caught the direction of her gaze. "It was time. But you understand, don't you? It was my own decision. No obligation on your part. I don't want you feeling responsible for anyone's actions but your own."

She nodded. It was the taking responsibility for her own actions she was still struggling with. Grieve for her mother. Grieve for the aborted baby. Come to acceptance. Move on. She understood the process. She just wasn't sure she had accomplished it. She'd done all she knew to do. But she kept feeling there should be something more. Maybe just give it time. They said time would heal, but she wasn't sure. If anything was festering, time would just make it worse, wouldn't it?

"Are you enjoying your book?"

She jumped at Greg's voice cutting across her thoughts. She looked at the discarded volume on the seat beside her. *The Power and the Glory.* She had thought she might read some on the drive, not realizing how preoccupied she would be with her own thoughts. "Yes, I am. It took me awhile to get into it. But as soon as I saw the symbolism of the priest riding a donkey, being hunted by the authorities, accused of being a wine-bibber, yet loving people everywhere he went, I was hooked."

"It's been years since I read it, but I remember being gripped by the picture of the suffering servant. Especially that scene where the priest offers his shirt to the man who was betraying him."

"Yes, I loved that too. And the police lieutenant who was such a zealous atheist. Let me see if I can find that part . . ." She flipped through the pages. "Oh, yes, here it is. Remember, he was watching the village children play: *They deserved nothing less than the truth—a vacant universe and a cooling world . . . He wanted to begin the world again with them, in a desert.* Isn't that the most powerful picture of a world without faith—a desert in a vacant universe, and a cooling world."

Greg nodded. "Gives you chills, doesn't it? And there was another part I liked—something about the image of God."

"Oh, yes. I read that yesterday." She turned several pages and scanned for a moment. "This is it. Where the government was destroying the statues in the cemetery: *It was odd—this fury to deface, because, of course, you could never deface enough. If God had been like a toad, you could have rid the globe of toads, but when God was like yourself, it was no good being content with stone figures—you had to kill yourself among the graves.*"

"Mmm, that's great." Then he was quiet.

Greg's silence was more companionable than most people's conversation. Then, since her book was open, Debbie read for a while. *Loving God isn't any different from loving a man—or a child. It's wanting to be with Him, to be near Him:* She was so absorbed in Greene's words it was a moment before she was aware that Greg had spoken. "Sorry. What?"

"I shouldn't have disturbed you. I just asked if you're excited about your interview?"

Well, it was a job. "Yeah, sure. I'll be fine." She looked

toward the city from the elevation of the freeway. Pearl gray skyscrapers, their windows reflecting the midmorning sun, rose from the richly wooded hills. "Portland's a beautiful city."

"It is. Hard to find your way around in it, though, because of all the bridges. We'll have to get you a good map. You'll soon catch on to it." He pointed to the south. "The seminary is about three miles over that way. It's a beautiful campus. Don't think we'll have time to go by it today, though. If I showed up, they'd probably try to put me to work."

"Is your home near there?"

"About three blocks from the campus. On a hillside with woods behind it." He took an exit that led along the river to a restored part of the old city and found a parking place under a bridge.

"It's great that they're redoing all these old buildings." Debbie looked around.

"I remember this area from when I was a kid—mostly just crumbling warehouses and dirty streets. You wouldn't believe it now, would you?" Freshly painted buildings were bordered with sidewalk planters filled with flourishing trees and flowers. "Several of these buildings have won Historic Preservation awards."

He escorted her toward the address she gave him. "I don't have to be at Parkinson's until this afternoon, so I'll just wait for you. Then we'll meet Courtenay for lunch."

In two blocks they reached the white stone building with awnings over the windows. Debbie recognized the displays of dresses made from original patterns, room furnishings such as chairs and light fixtures sewn from coordinating fabrics, and dozens of quilts and soft sculptures. Just like the Boise store, only larger. Not a bad place to start a career.

"There's a bookstore two doors down." Greg pointed. "I can browse for hours, so don't hurry." He squeezed her hand. "Good luck. You'll do great."

Rainbow Land was well named. It exuded color, joy, freshness, and creativity from all its displays. As Debbie waited for her interview, she could feel herself tingling with ideas: She'd love to make a quilt like that for Melissa, and those cut-out dolls—she could make one as a doll and appliqué the other on the front of a white pinafore and trim it in eyelet . . .

"You're Debbie? I'm Carol." The manager smiled and pushed her streaky blond hair away from her round face with the back of her hand. "Come in here where we can talk. You can see we need help—one girl quit and another is out sick today." She ushered Debbie into a small office, swept an armful of fabric samples off a chair, and indicated that Debbie should sit down.

They talked for less than half an hour, covering Debbie's fabric design education, her practical experience sewing, and her enthusiasm for working out her own creations with designer fabrics. Fortunately, they didn't dwell long on her inabilities with doing math calculations when selling four and three-fourths yards of fabric at $6.95 a yard and seven and two-thirds yards of ribbon at 56 cents a yard, and five-eighths of a yard of lace at . . .

Debbie finally got up her courage to ask, "Is there a chance I could work into a design job?"

"I can't promise. But I would hope so. We like to encourage creativity in our clerks."

Well, that was as much as Debbie could reasonably expect.

"I've only found one other applicant as qualified as you in three weeks of interviewing." Carol drew the meeting to a close. "And she really just wanted part-time work, so I think I can use you both. We're always so busy before Christmas, and it comes on so fast. When will you be able to start?"

"I hope to find an apartment this afternoon. If that goes well, shall we say a week from Monday?" It was all going so fast it took Debbie's breath away. She had the sensation of being on a train speeding through a dark tunnel.

Carol glanced at her calendar. "That's Labor Day. Let's make it Tuesday."

They shook hands, smiled at each other, and Debbie went out feeling as if she'd just been assigned a seat in the next tumbrel to the guillotine. *Ungrateful wretch,* she scolded herself all the way to the bookstore. *You couldn't ask for a better place to work. And you know it.*

They were to meet Courtenay for lunch at the nearby Pasta Faire, in one of the buildings Greg had mentioned as having won a preservation award. Wide, arched windows set in brick walls and billowy white, Austrian shaded light fixtures caught Debbie's eye, but then all her attention was taken by Greg's energetic sister. She was tall, her honey blond hair smartly cut, her businesslike camel blazer relieved of any hint of severity by the silky softness of her ivory blouse. She hugged them both warmly.

Debbie wondered what Greg had told his sister about her. Or did Courtenay greet all her clients like this? Courtenay gave their name to the maître d', then turned back. "Oh, I've longed for the beach this summer. But it was really important to Fred that we stay here just now, so—"

"You did the right thing." Greg smiled.

"Right thing for you, apparently." She looked at Debbie with a raised eyebrow. "And now with all the questions hanging over that Ryburg deal it looks as though the cottages might be there for us another year."

"Oh, your agency must have handled the sale of that property." Debbie had been so absorbed in the other things she had completely forgotten about Ryland Carlsburg and his business complications. "What's happening now?"

"Hard to say. The Ryburg people contend everything was aboveboard and proper and there's no reason not to proceed. All the talk of money under the table has raised some serious doubts, though." She looked at Greg. "Must be hard for you—with Gayle having been involved."

He shrugged. "It was a long time ago."

Courtenay looked skeptical. "Still, now that Melissa's old enough to understand, you wouldn't want any scandal to touch her."

"Nothing will touch Melissa." The harsh determination in his voice shocked Debbie.

Courtenay returned to her subject. "Anyway, last I heard Ryland Carlsburg had received all of his permits, so he's apparently plowing ahead."

"I suppose that's good for you," Debbie said.

"My commission, you mean? Well, yes. It should be the largest of my career. But money isn't everything. If my client had it to do over again, I'm not sure he'd agree to the sale. He's had those rentals for years and uses them for himself and his family members frequently. But then, Ryburg made him an offer he couldn't refuse—well over a million."

Debbie blinked. "For just the land?"

"That isn't just land. That's prime oceanfront property located in the fastest developing resort in the Pacific Northwest. I'd say Ryburg got a bargain."

A red-jacketed waiter motioned that their table was ready. After they were seated at a white linen-covered table next to a pedestal topped with a large arrangement of fern and tiger lilies, Debbie surveyed her menu while brother and sister caught up on family news. "And how is Melissa?" Courtenay asked.

"A new child. You'll have to see her to believe it."

"That's an answer to prayer."

"I hope so." The tentative tone in his voice puzzled Debbie. But then the waiter approached for their orders. Debbie chose spinach salad with smoked salmon and angel hair pasta.

While they ate Courtenay produced a notebook and ran down the list of possibilities in rental apartments. "In the price range Greg said you might want, the five at the top look the best. They all have easy access to downtown. I've arranged for us to see them if they sound good to you, so we'll have a busy afternoon."

"Thank you so much. I'd be absolutely lost without your help." Actually, Debbie was coming to terms with her reluctance. She wasn't feeling so much lost as carried along by events beyond her control. It was a surprisingly comfortable feeling. She had always felt she had to be in control. Control of her environment, of the people around her, of her life. The sense of being able to loosen her grip on the reins was so relaxing.

Greg glanced at his watch and asked for the check. "I've got to run. Hugh Parkinson does not like to be kept waiting. Debbie," he turned to her. "I've got someplace really special I want to show you this evening. Something important. Courtenay will take you, and I'll meet you there."

"OK." She didn't even ask him what or where.

The first apartment was large with a cathedral ceiling in the living room and the bedroom in a loft. The building offered a swimming pool and recreation room. Debbie shook her head. "This would definitely stretch the budget past the breaking point."

The next offering had a lot of genteel, shabby charm and definite possibilities for being fixed up. Unfortunately, the neighborhood was not one in which Debbie felt comfortable.

The third was attractively priced, but Debbie was chilled by the ice blue interior and northern exposure. "Brr, it's bad enough on a sunny afternoon. Can you imagine it on a rainy winter day?" Debbie's sense of relaxation was turning to plain old fatigue. And even the indefatigable Courtenay walked a bit slower.

They drove out Barber Boulevard toward the university. "This is a beautiful area." Debbie looked at the banks of ivy tangling up the hillside beneath dark green Douglas firs.

"Wait till we get up here a bit further. On a clear day like this we should have a spectacular view of Mount Hood."

Courtenay had no more than finished speaking when she turned down a drive and Mount Hood rose in the distance, proud and solitary, the sun shining on the pristine whiteness of her peak. The hillside Debbie stood on when she got out of the car was a tangled mass of bank upon bank of verdant greenery, fresh from its recent watering by a gentle Portland rain. "You can't imagine how good all this green looks to a girl raised in the desert," she said.

"It is beautiful. But it won't take you long to figure out why they call the Oregon football team the Ducks." Courtenay laughed and led the way into a small apartment that looked out on the view they were just admiring.

Debbie looked around at the soft lemon walls and serviceable brown furniture. Hmm, unbleached muslin curtains, hunter green and cranberry accents—that was what it needed. "Surely nothing with a view like this could be in my price range."

"It's a sublease. A definite bargain, but only available for nine months. That's why I didn't bring you here sooner. I didn't think you'd want anything so temporary."

Debbie shrugged. "It's the right place. I'll worry about the next step when I get there." Her own words shocked her. Since when had Deborah Jensen been willing to take things one step at a time? What had happened to her desperate need to control everything?

Courtenay looked at her watch. "Good thing we don't need to look at that last one. I've just got time to deliver you to Gregory." She led the way to the car.

"What is this place Greg was so mysterious about?"

"The Grotto? It's a really special garden. I don't know why the mystery, but I'm sure you'll enjoy it."

They turned off Sandy Boulevard by a large white sign that said Sanctuary of Our Sorrowful Mother. As soon as they pulled into the parking lot Debbie saw Greg get out of his car and walk toward them. They told Courtenay goodbye and turned toward the sanctuary. Just inside the tall white fence they found a bench under a wide-spreading tree. "Let me explain." Greg sat at the far end of the bench, not touching her. "But first, tell me how you're feeling about things."

Debbie considered. "Better. Amazingly better. But—" She paused. "I guess I'd say not finished. I've done everything I can think of: prayed, mailed the letter to Shawn, called Dad and the twins . . ." She shrugged. "But it just feels like there should be something more."

He nodded. "That's what I thought. That's why I wanted you to come here. You never really grieved for your mother or for your child."

Debbie shook her head. "I've cried more these past six days than in the whole six years before. And it has helped. It's an amazing release. Relaxing."

"That's right. That's what grieving is all about. God made us that way. Short-circuiting that part of our nature will be as disastrous as ignoring any of God's other principles. But I think you've left out one part of the process."

"What's that?" Just the suggestion that there was something more she could do was wonderful news. Now that she had begun to recover, Debbie didn't want to stop anywhere short of complete wellness.

"You need to say good-bye."

"I don't understand."

"One of the reasons you feel so abandoned by your mother is that you didn't see her in the hospital."

"I abandoned her." Debbie choked. The tears were coming again.

"The whole experience gets jumbled up inside. It comes to the same thing. If you could have been with her when she died, you would have felt much better. Families who lose loved ones in wars or airplane crashes where the bodies aren't recovered have a much harder time grieving than those who can go to a mortuary with an open casket."

Debbie shook her head. "I didn't look in the casket. I

went to the funeral, but I shut my eyes and my mind."

Greg nodded. "And, of course, there was no funeral for your baby."

"They told me it was just a cell mass. Like having my tonsils out. You don't have a funeral for your tonsils. I didn't really believe them, but I tried to."

"Come on." Greg stood and held out his hand. "This is an international shrine to motherhood. I can't think of a better place to say your good-byes."

They walked slowly, hand-in-hand, down a wooded path. Debbie felt the peaceful solitude of the natural beauty permeate her soul. Even the birdsongs seemed hushed. She was thankful for a companion who understood the beauty of silence. Beneath the tall, straight pines and filigree birch trees, banks of fern, ivy, and flowering shrubs grew in profusion. Tucked in among the plants and mossy rocks, looking as natural as if they had grown there, were pieces of religious art to help the viewer focus on the Creator of all the surrounding beauty.

As they approached the Grotto, soft organ strains floated on the air. At the base of a sheer rock cliff a cave with a gothic-arched opening formed a natural altar. Inside the cave stood a white marble replica of Michelangelo's *Pietà*. Debbie let go of Greg's hand and walked forward toward the altar. She felt drawn to kneel. Love engulfed her.

Flickering candles amid the ferns and the soft evening light made Mary's face glow with a mother's love and sorrow as she held her Son on her lap. Debbie could think only of her own mother holding her, looking at her with a similar love. And her arms ached to so hold the child she never knew.

Even as her pain to be embraced by her mother and to give a mother's embrace grew she found a satisfaction in experiencing the pain. It was a good ache. Normal. Healthy. And she could sense a healing in the process of closing her eyes and imagining herself on her mother's lap, feeling her mother's arms holding her. She once again experienced her dream of her mother coming to her. She could experience being a child again in her mother's arms, warmed after being out in the rain.

And even as she felt her mother's arms around her, she felt the tiny sweet baby in her own arms. As her tears fell on her empty lap her aching arms felt comforted, almost—almost holy as she offered her baby to God's care.

She was hardly aware of Greg leading her to a small garden beyond the Grotto. High hedges enclosed it like a tiny chapel. The air smelled of roses. A statue stood in the center. Mary holding the Christ child. Banks of flowers behind her.

And then the scene shifted in Debbie's mind. Her mother stood there. She smiled and held out her arms. Debbie walked to her, aware of the tender, warm weight in her own arms. Debbie placed the precious life she carried in her mother's arms.

She didn't know how long she stayed there. She couldn't remember whether she had stood or knelt. The experience of being there with her mother and her baby were a foretaste of heaven. She had the comfort of knowing her two dear ones were together now. And she would be with them one day.

When she returned to Greg it was sunset. He led the way to an elevator that took them to the top of a cliff. In the soft dusk they strolled through the monastery rose garden, the scent of beauty heavy on the evening air. Peace roses grew in exotic profusion. Debbie cupped a blossom so large it filled both her hands. A golden glow came from the depths of the flower, as if it contained its own light, then shaded to a delicate ivory, turning to a blush of pink edging. The petals felt baby-skin velvet to her fingers. Peace. *I give you my peace.*

She hadn't thought such serenity could be possible for her.

She offered her hand to Greg. They walked to the edge

of the garden. The view was magnificent, a panoramic scope across the wide Columbia River. The sky reflected the same glowing gold, delicate ivory, and blush pink as the rose petals. The evening breeze swept across her with a sense of freshness and newness. The world was a perfect reflection of what she felt inside. Clean. Refreshed. Renewed. Old things passed away. All things become new.

Chapter 17

Debbie slept late that morning with the peace of a newborn baby and awoke with the feeling that this was the first day of the rest of her life. She sang as she stirred orange juice and toasted a muffin, thinking about the two next door who were so very dear to her. What were they doing? Were they still asleep? She couldn't wait to finish breakfast and run see them. She wanted to hold Melissa. Take her on her lap and enfold her in her arms, just as in all the tangled mother-child images she had worked through yesterday. Only today it would be a real, live child filling the void in her arms.

And Greg. He could take her in his arms. Not as a replacement of her mother or anything she had lost in the past but as a promise for the future. And then she thought. Greg had been so very quiet last night. He had said hardly a word on the whole drive from Portland. Of course it had been late. An incredibly long day. And she had thought he had just been respecting her feelings, giving her time to continue working through the miracle of newness in her life.

But now she wondered.

No, don't be silly. Greg was always undemanding, never pushing. Today they could spend hours talking about it all. And about the future if he chose to. She wouldn't push, either. But now she was free to think ahead. For once in her life she left the dirty dishes in the sink and ran out, letting the screen door slam behind her.

At first she didn't see the note stuck in the doorframe. Then she almost didn't look at it. How could it be for her? Why would Greg be leaving her a note? She looked at her name on the envelope a second time to be sure, a cold feeling creeping over her. The cottage was too quiet. She looked around. His car wasn't in the parking lot. She ripped the envelope open.

Debbie gripped the rail and sank to the top step, clutching the two sheets of paper. What did the words mean? Gone to Portland. Emergency. Hope you understand. Will see you when you move to your apartment. I can get the address from Courtenay.

She blinked and looked again. *Emergency.* Melissa? Was Melissa suddenly taken ill? Complications with the appendectomy? But no, Melissa had drawn her a happy picture of herself standing under a rainbow, waving, with a row of pink flowers across the front and a bright yellow sunshine in the corner. Melissa was fine.

Hope you understand. Understand what? How could she possibly understand when he had told her nothing?

See you when you move? Not till then? He won't call?

Address from Courtenay. Don't try to contact me. I'll contact you. If I decide to. She let the papers fall to the ground. Maybe she did understand. She had been a case study. A medical challenge, so to speak. And he had won. Case closed.

She should have realized . . . She did realize all along, didn't she? It was easy enough for him to accept her as a therapy patient. But accepting her as a wife and mother—after he knew the full story—was quite a different matter.

He had been absolutely right in all his counseling. And she was grateful. She would always be grateful. And she had always known, hadn't she? She had always known, but tried to convince herself otherwise, that she wasn't good enough for Gregory Masefield. Now he realized it too. She could see that at first he might think her the perfect woman: she had all the homemaking skills that Gayle had so despised; she adored Melissa and Melissa adored her; and she and Greg had become so close—so very close—as he metaphorically held her hand while she worked through all her trauma.

But now the counseling was over. Now he could look at her as a woman, not a patient, and he saw how far his perfect woman was from being all he had thought. Could she expect any man of character to accept an aborted woman as a mother for his own child? If he took her in his arms, would Shawn be between them?

He had done all he could to help her. Now she had to face the question of going forward. Alone. And the fear almost overwhelmed her. The fear that losing Greg—and Melissa—was going to be as major a trauma in her life as her past mistakes had been. How could she go on?

"Yo, Deb!" Byrl stuck her head out the kitchen door and waved. "Telephone."

She jumped up so fast she almost fell down the steps. He did call! Of course he would. How could she have doubted him? Greg wouldn't just go off like that. That was why he didn't explain, because he was planning to call. He probably thought he would talk to her before she even saw that silly note. She was so relieved she laughed out loud.

"Hello!"

"Well, hello, gorgeous. You sound happy. Can I take that as a good omen?"

She was so shocked she pulled the receiver from her ear. "What? Who—"

"Hey, it's Ryland. Don't tell me I've been gone so long you've forgotten me?"

"Er—"

"Well, that's what I get for putting business before pleasure. But I'm determined to make up for lost time. And we've got some celebrating to do."

"Oh?"

"That's right, Baby. The deal is in the bag. Got the last form filled out and filed yesterday. I tell you, we could build that whole hotel out of the triplicate forms and red tape I had to wade through, but it's done."

"Er, what about Mrs. Larsen's group?"

"Hey, no problem. She's a sweet, well-meaning lady, what can I say? Doesn't quite understand how things work in the real world, but sweet. Very sweet. But we're wasting time. Put your glad rags on—something sunny and sexy. I'm picking you up in an hour."

Sunny and sexy? She didn't own anything like that. And she wouldn't have worn it for Ryland Carlsburg if she had. But she didn't really have anything else to do. She could already hear Byrl's computer clicking away. And she had no desire to wash dishes or sew at the moment. In the end she put on a soft, wraparound skirt and knit top.

She was almost ready when Byrl emerged. "Oh, going out with Adonis?"

Debbie shook her head. "That was Ryland on the phone. I'm going out with him."

"*Oh.*" Byrl bit her lip.

"*Oh,* what?"

"Well, I didn't know whether or not to tell you, but I think you need to know. Margaret Larsen really does have a lot on him and—" she paused. "Well, you'll learn about it soon enough. It looks like Gayle Masefield was involved up to her eyebrows."

"Oh, dear."

"Duane Larsen was going to take it to the press just before he died. I've asked her to hold off—at least until Greg leaves Seaside—but the story will go statewide. I thought you should be warned."

Ryland's little black sports car pulled into the driveway. "Thanks for telling me, Byrl. We'll talk more later."

Ryland drove down the coast to the Crab Broiler. The natural wood interior decorated with green plants was refreshing, and the stuffed crab thermidor served in the shell was exquisite, but Debbie hardly noticed. She had determined to put Greg out of her mind. At least for the moment. But the things Byrl had told her kept pushing at her. And she might as well focus on Ryland's business deals as anything else. It seemed she had been involved from the sidelines all summer, so she was interested in how it had all turned out. She phrased her question obliquely, not wanting to accuse her host or Greg's wife. But Ryland hooted at her question.

"Bribery! Of course there were charges of bribery. There always are by the side that loses." He took a sip of his iced tea, regarding her over the rim of his glass. "You're such an innocent. That's probably one of the things I find most attractive about you. But you are making an enormous issue out of something that is no more than standard business practice. Lobbying elected officials is part of the American system."

Debbie wanted to ask where he would draw the line between lobbying and bribing, but she let it go. "OK, so you obtained the license without corrupt practices, but can you really deny that the whole gambling industry reeks of corruption?"

"Of course I deny it. You've been watching too many gangster movies. Why shouldn't the West Coast have an Atlantic City?"

The rest of the crab thermidor disappeared somewhere between arguments over organized crime, law enforcement costs, and promoting compulsive gambling versus increased local jobs, enhancing tourism, and expanded recreation. At last Ryland tossed his napkin onto the table. "Ah, that's what I like. Good, stimulating discussion over a meal. It's good for digestion, you know. But, Deb, you're too uptight. You've got to learn to relax and have fun. That's what a casino is all about—people having fun. But since mine isn't built yet, I can't show you; so I have an alternate plan." He held her chair for her to get up, opened the restaurant door, then held the door of his sleek sports car—all with a flourish.

He put a CD of romantic show tunes on the player built into his dashboard and drove up a thickly wooded, little-used road toward Tillamook Head. The music was light, the scenery soothing. Debbie began to relax. They chatted casually, Ryland interspersing his conversation with jokes. He really could be very witty. Very fun to be with. The road wound steeply upward, the vegetation becoming more thickly verdant. Debbie commented on the beauty of the banks of dark yellow flowers along the road.

Ryland assented, but unfortunately, that made her think again of the environmental issues of his development. And the other problems surrounding it. "If it's all such an aboveboard, fun thing, why did you keep your plans so hush-hush?"

The car jerked. Muttering an expletive under his breath, Ryland pulled to the side of the road and turned off the motor. "There were sound business reasons for what I did. None of which I feel compelled to explain to you at the moment. But there is something else I feel a very strong compulsion to do."

Before Debbie even realized what was happening, Ryland pulled her into his arms and began kissing her urgently. She was so shocked it was a moment before she reacted, then she pushed hard with her hands flat against the starched white shirt front. "What do you think you're doing?"

Ryland chuckled. "I knew you were an innocent, but I didn't expect it to go that far. It's called a kiss—something two people—"

"Something two people do when they care deeply for one another. Not when one of them wants to win a political argument."

"Innocent. And wrong too. That's not what I kissed you for, but it has been known to work. As a matter of fact, my construction foreman quite recently used it very effectively on a highly placed female administrative assistant."

Debbie blinked. The woman Byrl saw in Alex's room?

"And now I've shocked you again. What a day this has been. You wouldn't believe what our Alex has been up to. Matter of fact, I just got off the phone with him before I picked you up. Afraid he's rather overstepped his bounds. I had to sack him. Pity, he's a useful fellow, but he was getting above himself. Sorry, my dear, didn't mean to bore you with business. Now, to get back to us, I want to be absolutely, soul-baringly honest—"

"Is that possible?"

He passed over her jibe with a raised eyebrow. "The fact of the matter is that although I've wanted to kiss you ever since I met you at Hugh Parkinson's party, the reason I stopped just now is that I think we have a tire going flat."

"Well, at least that's a little more original than the run-ning-out-of-gas gambit." Debbie folded her arms and leaned back in the seat. "So why aren't you out fixing it?"

"Right." He yanked his door open, but waited to get out until an old blue pickup, the only vehicle they had seen since turning up the mountain trail, lumbered past them and on down the dirt road. "Now, don't bounce around any when I get this thing up on the jack or you'll have to get out. But you better roll the windows down for a little fresh air."

Fresh air was definitely what she needed. Fresh air to blow away the clammy feel of Ryland's hands on her arms and his lips on her mouth. One idea of hers had certainly backfired. Ryland was no defense against missing Greg. Nothing she could possibly experience could show her more vividly how much more she wanted to be with Greg than with any other man.

What she really wanted was a good wash. The old de-sire returned to plunge neck-deep into a hot, soapy tub of water, to wash her hair and scrub her hands over and over. But that wasn't possible here. The best she could do was to put her head out the open window and take a deep gulp of piney forest air.

Unfortunately, the effect was not soothing. The pungent odor of the yellow wildflowers blooming in profusion by the roadside tickled her nose. A violent fit of sneezing ensued.

Sniffing loudly and dabbing at her eyes with the back of

her hand, Debbie dug in her pocket for a hanky. She didn't have one. And she felt another round of sneezing coming on. In desperation she opened the glove compartment before her. A package of tissues almost fell in her lap. She pulled one out and mopped at her streaming eyes and nose.

She was just replacing the package when Ryland cranked the jack down rapidly. The car settled onto the road with a jolt. The papers in the glove box slid out and fell to the floor. Debbie fumbled for them, pushed them into a pile, and reached to replace them. Then she froze. What was that? there—in the bottom of the compartment?

An airplane control.

But surely not the same one. She leaned forward for a closer inspection. It still had bits of sand clinging to it. Was this, as she suspected, the second control box, used to override Larsen's and plunge the plane into his head? Ryland hadn't returned it as he promised. The slamming trunk lid told her he was coming. She jammed the papers and tissues in the glove box and closed it just as he got into the car. The square of black plastic she edged into the deep pocket of her skirt.

Her mind whirled. *There could be an explanation. Surely. He'd been out of town. Maybe he forgot. Maybe he's still going to do it. Maybe . . .*

She had to know. "Ryland, I never heard what became of that radio control for the Larsens' airplane we found. Did you get it back to them OK?"

He started the car. "Yeah, sure. The kid—er, Rick, I think his name is—was real glad to get it back. Said he knew he'd dropped it somewhere, but of course hadn't had a chance to go back and look."

"You gave it to him personally?"

"Yeah. Before I went to Salem. The fact that his mom was leading a campaign against me was no reason not to be nice to the kid."

He chatted on, but Debbie wasn't listening. She was too

busy watching it all again in her mind: father and son flying the soaring model, the freak behavior of the plane, the horror of the blood on the sand, and something she hadn't thought about before—Ryland Carlsburg walking to her through the crowd—from the far side of the dune. From precisely the spot she had found the control buried in the sand the next morning. Was that why Ryland was out there at the same place so early the next morning? To retrieve the incriminating evidence he knew he'd left behind? Had he dropped it by mistake? Or buried it because he didn't want to take a chance of having it discovered on him?

Was she being driven along a deserted mountain trail by a murderer?

But in the next heartbeat her mind conjured up another, far more alarming, scene. Gregory, running to her from the far side of that same dune—when he had supposedly been out on the beach.

She tried to pray. But she was so frozen with horror and confusion that words wouldn't form in her mind. Just sit here quietly, she told herself. Try to sort it out. Act like nothing's happened. Don't give it away that you know anything. When you get back to town you can take it to the police. Let them work it out.

Even if it was Greg? Was it possible that sheltering Melissa from scandal was important enough to him that he tried to discourage Larsen? Not kill him. She could never believe that—but just keep him out of the way for a while—and then the whole thing had gone terribly wrong? Greg *had* demonstrated his skill at remote flying with the stunt kite. Could that have been a warm-up exercise? She shook her head.

As impossible as it was to think that Gregory Masefield could be involved in anything shady, it was even more impossible to think of Melissa being hurt. But yes, even if, incredibly, Greg was involved, the truth had to be known. Debbie had suffered too much in her own life from keeping the truth hidden.

Her hand brushed her pocket where the control made an awkward bulge. And that action brought such relief she almost shouted. Of course it wasn't Greg. Ryland was the one who had lied about the control. And they couldn't possibly be working together. No, not even for Melissa's sake, Greg wouldn't.

". . . So what do you say to that?"

She jumped. She hadn't heard a word he'd said. "What? Sorry. I wasn't following."

"I must say, that's not very flattering. Most women would jump at an invitation to cocktails and dancing on a yacht at sunset." He glanced at his watch. "We've just got time to make it." He pushed the gas pedal down in spite of the roughness of the road.

"No. I can't really, Ryland. I have plans this evening. I promised Byrl. I can't. No." She knew she was babbling. Sweat broke out on her forehead. Why wasn't she a better actress? Ryland would see her desperation. He would guess she knew. She had to get away.

And then the words were out of her mouth before she realized she had spoken. "Ryland, stop!"

"What?"

She spoke with a calm she could only wish she felt. "Stop the car. Please. I have to, er—well, just be a gentleman and stop."

He grinned at her. "Anything you say. Drank too much iced tea, did you?"

She forced herself to walk slowly until she was sure she was out of sight of the car. Then all pretense of calm left her as she began running wildly, blindly, propelled by nothing but sheer animal terror.

There was no path. She wouldn't have dared use one if there had been. How long would Ryland wait in the car before he realized something was wrong? Would he guess what had happened? Look in the glove compartment and learn what she had with her?

Debbie dodged bushes, tree stumps, low branches, trying to make as much speed as possible without injuring herself. And there was the need to be quiet. Noises could carry great distances in the woods. If he came after her, his long legs and greater strength could make much better time than she, especially if he had the sound of her trailblazing to follow.

She crawled over a fallen, decaying tree and lay still for a moment in the soft grass beside it. All she could hear was the pounding of her heart.

She pushed herself to her feet and went on. She had no idea where she was going, but she reasoned that if she continued downhill she would eventually come to the town or highway or somewhere she could get help.

Her skirt caught on a ragged stump, forcing her to halt her flight. And then she heard it—the unmistakable sound of someone crashing through the woods behind her. Was he even calling her name? She yanked. Her skirt came free with a ripping sound. She rushed wildly on, unsure how much longer her burning lungs and aching legs could keep up the pace.

But it didn't really matter how long she could keep on because the noise behind her was getting closer every second. She shot a look over her shoulder and thought she caught a glimpse of his white shirt through the branches. She must keep on as long as she could. "Debbie!" Her heart was pounding so hard, her breathing so raspy she could barely recognize her own name.

Faster. She had to go faster. She plunged, misjudged the height of a low-hanging pine branch and ran face-first into a clump of stinging needles. She reeled back, lost her balance, and slammed into a granite boulder. That was the last thing she remembered.

Chapter 18

Debbie struggled against the darkness holding her down. If only she could get her eyes open, the darkness would go away and take her headache with it. She started to blink, but the effort was too great. She sank again into the blackness.

"Debbie!" A man's voice was calling her. Why was he so far away? If he'd come closer, maybe she could answer him.

"Debbie!" Was that Ryland? Why didn't he just strangle her and get it over with? She tried to turn away from him, but the effort was too great. She had lost. A man who had killed once wouldn't hesitate to do it again.

"Debbie!" She felt his hands on her.

She tried to struggle. "No!"

"Open your eyes." The command was accompanied with a firm shake.

She struggled to obey the command. She opened them just enough to see the white shirt. Danger. The white shirt meant danger. She had been running from a white shirt.

"She's coming around. Over here, Charlie!"

Again she opened her eyes just enough to see the white shirt, this time from the back. Something was wrong . . . Her eyelids shut again. Then snapped open. The head above the shirt was blond.

"Greg?"

"Oh, thank God." He came to her bed. "Don't sit up yet."

"All right. But I'm OK. Except for the headache." It did feel good, though, to lie there with her eyes closed. Greg would take care of everything. *Greg?* Greg was here? Then did that mean— No, it couldn't. She would never believe he was capable of working with Ryland. Yet she had to know. "Greg! What are you doing here?"

"It's a long story. Quick version is that Charlie here had been fixing a leaky pipe in a cabin on the mountain. He saw you by the side of the road with Ryland. Didn't think you looked very happy about the situation, so he told me."

"But he couldn't have. You weren't there." Now she remembered. That was why she had gone with Ryland in the first place. She struggled to an upright position, in spite of the swirling blackness that threatened to overwhelm her. "You left. I went over and you were gone. You just—"

"Shh." He put a finger gently on her lips. "Don't upset yourself. I'll explain everything. Later, when you feel better."

"But *how* did you get there? Were you the white shirt I was running from? Where's Ryland?" Now she opened her eyes wide and looked around. "Where are we?"

"One thing at a time. In reverse. We're at the hospital. Emergency room. You had a really bad crack on your head."

She put her hand to the back of her head. She hadn't realized it was bandaged. She prodded with her fingers, then groaned.

"Ryland is with the police. Yes, you were running from me. I yelled and yelled, but you didn't seem to hear me."

She shook her head. All she had heard was her own panic—in such confusion that she might have kept running even if she had realized it was Greg. "Police? Do they know he murdered Larsen? I have the control. I found it in his car." She reached to her pocket. "It's gone!"

"Nurse found it when I brought you in. Police have it now."

"But how did they know?"

"I called them, before I headed up the hill with Charlie." He sighed and sat on the edge of her bed. "OK, I was going to wait until you felt better, but the bare bones of it are this: I was going to Portland. We'll talk about that later. I stopped for some coffee at a drive-through espresso place. That foreman of Carlsburg's that Byrl used to date was there—owns the place, actually. He had just got off the phone with Carlsburg and was really steamed. He told me all about it because of Gayle. Carlsburg had fired him. Just like that, over the phone. Just like he had fired Gayle the night of her accident."

"Carlsburg fired Gayle?"

Greg nodded. "She had refused to go along with his tactics. Alex made some extravagant accusation about Carlsburg having engineered her accident. A drugged drink or something." He ran a hand through his hair. "We'll never know."

Through all the tangled tale, one thing was clear. "Greg, that clears Gayle, doesn't it?"

"That's right."

"I'm so glad. So glad." She struggled to sit up, but dizziness held her down. "So what about Alex?"

"He was afraid Carlsburg would try to pin Larsen's murder on him. He was talking pretty wild, but the things he said made enough sense, combined with what I knew. I got right in the car and drove straight back to Seaside." He took her hand. "A decision for which I'll be eternally grateful."

"Mmmm." Debbie wanted to say, "Me too," but words were suddenly too much effort.

A brisk young doctor came in and examined her. He prescribed ice for her bump, aspirin for her headache, and a nice long rest. They were in Greg's car, almost back to the cottage, when she asked, "But why did he keep it—the airplane control?"

"Alex is convinced that Carlsburg was planning to use it to frame him if the police got too close."

Debbie leaned back and closed her eyes. She didn't want to talk about Ryland Carlsburg. She wanted to talk about Greg and her. But her head still ached. And the medication they had given her at the hospital was taking effect. Greg all but carried her into the cottage, and Byrl tucked her in bed.

She was just drifting off to sleep when a thought jolted her awake. It was too dark to see anything in her room, but she stretched her eyes open anyway, aching to see. As if physical sight could show her what she sought. Greg had not said one word about *them.*

Because he was there—because he had miraculously come back—she thought he had come back to *her.* But now she realized, he had said no such thing. He had come back to get the police. If Charlie hadn't taken Greg up to Tillamook Head, he would probably just have turned around and gone back to Portland. And she would never have seen him again.

Maybe she never would see him again. She struggled to get out of bed, but headache and medication overcame her.

Chapter 19

Physically, Debbie felt much better the next morning. Emotionally, she was still numb. But no matter, she was not going to lie in bed any longer. Whatever the day was to bring, she would be ready for it.

She removed the bandage and washed her hair, taking her time about getting ready. Ready for what? She suddenly realized that everything was over. The lease on the cottage would be up in a few days. The business with Ryland was in the hands of the police. And Greg and Melissa were going back to Portland.

She had experienced a sense of new beginnings standing on the cliff over the Columbia. But she had had no idea how new. Next Tuesday she would be starting an entirely new life. She almost felt she should change her name to symbolize the new person she had become.

She walked out on the beach. It was a soft morning. Not really foggy or rainy, just a soft-focus lens on the world. And she was alone. Yet not alone. God was there.

And for the first time in years, she found that was not a fearsome thought. She could hold out her arms as if to embrace Him with no fear of His judgment. There was now no need to hide from Him, thinking she had committed the unpardonable sin. All those years of believing that there was forgiveness for everybody else but not for her, all that time hoping she had salvation for dying, but knowing she had none for living, it all melted in a wonderful sense of His presence, His grace that extended even to her.

But it was more than forgiveness, more than assurance, more than freedom. It was—it was love. There, in that moment, she fell in love. Just as she had fallen in love with Greg, and yet far more profoundly, more gloriously. She was in love with Jesus Christ.

Yes! She wanted to shout and sing. She wanted to embrace the universe. She wanted to tell Greg. She turned and started toward his cottage, light with joy. Then she stopped. What if he wasn't there? What if he had gone again?

She stood, thinking. What if there was to be no more of Gregory Masefield in her life? She would miss him terribly, that was certain. She had never before known anyone she so wanted to share every moment of her life with as she did Greg. The thought of going on without him was a physical pain. An unbearable weight in her chest.

Yet even as she gasped at the hurt, she knew that if he was gone she would survive. She had Another with her who would never leave her. She thought He had. For six years she thought He was no longer there. But she knew now that He had never left her for a moment. And never would.

So she would never be alone.

She moved forward.

Her footsteps sounded hollow on the wooden steps to Greg's back door. And her knock was equally hollow. Just as she had expected, there was no answer. He was gone. This time without even leaving a note.

She walked back to the cottage. Slowly. Not smiling. But with her head up.

She had taken two steps inside the living room when a small pink form flung itself into her arms. "Hooray, you're here! We've come to ask you to marry us!"

Debbie staggered to the nearest chair and collapsed with Melissa in her arms. She looked around the room, speechless.

Byrl rescued her. "Come on, kid-o, let her catch her breath." She pulled the child off Debbie.

Greg strode across the room and sat in the chair next to her. "Sorry. That wasn't very subtle. She got a bit ahead of me."

Byrl took a firm grip on Melissa's hand. "Come on. We'll go feed the seals."

"But, Daddy, can't I give her the present first? Please?"

Greg threw up his hands. "I didn't plan it this way." He looked pleadingly at Debbie.

Debbie grinned and took the elegantly wrapped box from Melissa. She looked at Greg, questioning.

"Go ahead, open it." He smiled and shrugged, apparently resigned to his fate.

Debbie's fingers trembled as she pulled the blue satin bow off the package. The only noise in the room was of her fumbling with the pale blue tissue paper inside. Then her cry of delight. The Cybis *Birth of Venus* emerged from her bed of foam.

"It's 'someday'; it's 'someday'!" Melissa bounced up and down, clapping her hands.

"You remembered," Debbie whispered, looking at Greg and shaking her head in amazement. She held the precious figure in her hand. Its beauty, its delicacy, its symbolism of birth—the birth of love, the birth of a new life—overwhelmed her. She caressed the porcelain with her finger. It was soft as velvet, warm, almost living. And it was from Greg.

"Come on. Those seals are going to starve." Byrl drug Melissa from the room.

And then Debbie saw what she hadn't noticed before. Nestled in the curve of a shell beside the goddess's bare foot was a ring. A perfect pearl embedded in a band of wrought gold. She held it out. "Greg?"

He hesitated before he answered. "Everything has happened so fast. It's been more like watching a movie than really living. We still need time. Normal, day-to-day time. You need time and space to enjoy the new you. But I wanted something—some symbol of commitment. That's why I got a pearl rather than a diamond."

"I love it. It's perfect. But—?" she still didn't understand.

Greg slipped to his knees beside her. "Forgive me for going off like that yesterday. I just had to think everything through. I had to be sure—for all our sakes."

Debbie looked at him, trying to understand what he was saying.

"I had to find my own heart—after concentrating so hard on yours. I had to be sure I wasn't in love with a dream version of my ideal."

"But you know how very far from ideal I am."

"And I know how far from perfect I am. And I know we have to live a real life together—not something from one of my textbooks. I had to be sure that we—with God's help—could make it work."

"And?"

"I'm sure. Every mile I got further away the surer I was. Can you forgive me for going off like that?" She started to answer, but he stopped her. "Let me try to explain."

"You don't have to explain, Greg."

"Yes I do. To myself, if not to you. I had put my own feelings and desires aside. The important thing was that you get well. I was just so thankful that I could help you. And all the time I had kept at the back of my mind the thought that once that was over—when you were firmly established in your recovery—then there would be time. Time then to quit being Dr. Gregory Masefield, theologian and counselor, and be Greg Masefield, the man. I had been longing for that moment for weeks . . ."

"And then it came and you weren't so sure."

He stood and ran his fingers through his hair. "I was frightened. Incredibly, I had found you—the perfect woman. I hadn't thought it possible, but I had." He paused. "No, I couldn't take any of the credit. It was all grace. God had dropped you in my lap . . ."

Debbie nodded. She knew what he was building up to. "And then you took a good look at how imperfect I am. I know, Greg."

He shook his head and knelt by her again. "I hated myself for feeling that way. I told myself I was being legalistic, judgmental, unloving . . . But I knew ignoring my honest reactions would only lead to disaster. Nothing in my counseling study had prepared me for that. I had waited, and then, when I could at last take you in my arms without inhibition . . . Then I found myself turning away. Running, even." He was quiet for a long moment. "And I almost lost you."

She put her hand on his arm. "Don't be so hard on yourself. You married once for infatuation. You had to be certain what you were doing this time." He looked at the ring, then at her hand. "And you? Are you sure?"

She gave him a small smile and nodded. "The old Debbie was never sure of anything. This one is very sure."

He slipped the ring on her finger and took her in his arms. His kiss was the first one in a world made new.

The Beginning

For Further Reading

Selby, Terry L., with Marc Bockmon. *The Mourning After, Help for the Postabortion Syndrome*. Grand Rapids: Baker Book House, 1990.

Quotations and Retellings From

Greene, Graham. *The Power and the Glory*. London: Heinemann, 1940.

Potter, Beatrix. *The Tale of Peter Rabbit*. London: Frederick Warne and Co., 1902.

Stevenson, Robert Louis. "The Swing," in *A Child's Garden of Verses*. London, 1885.

Acknowledgments

Thank you to Terry Selby, M.S.W., and Dr. Thomas Tilden, M.D., F.A.A.P., for consultations and research assistance.